"Lucy tells me you've been having some problems with the house . . ."

"Problems?" Stephanie felt her control slipping. It wasn't her strong suit to begin with. "Two weeks after I moved in, the front porch rotted out from under me. Then the water heater blew up and flooded the cellar. None of the windows will open, and it's hotter than heck in—" She stopped when she saw the smile spread across his face. "Something funny about a water heater exploding?"

Ivan didn't think there was anything funny about a water heater exploding, and he couldn't understand how so many things could go wrong with his house. He'd left it in perfect condition. He loved Haben. It had belonged to his family for generations, and he would never have sold it if it hadn't been absolutely necessary. He was smiling despite everything because Stephanie Lowe was a sight that inspired smiles.

"I think you're cute when you get all steamed up," he admitted, playfully patting her cowlick. "Why is your hair sticking up? Is this a new style?"

Stephanie felt the top of her head. "When the upstairs toilet broke, it leaked onto the floor and collapsed the ceiling in the kitchen and downstairs bathroom. When the ceiling fell down in the bathroom, it took the mirrored door off the medicine chest and smashed it on the sink. Since that was the only mirror in the house, I had to comb my hair in front of the toaster."

Ivan _____ at her. Maybe she's a wacko and making _____ _____ _____ _____ od that she was wa____ _____ _____ _____ .

Books by Janet Evanovich

Manhunt
Metro Girl
Back to the Bedroom
Love Overboard
The Rocky Road to Romance

One for the Money
Two for the Dough
Three to Get Deadly
Four to Score
High Five
Hot Six
Seven Up
Hard Eight
Visions of Sugar Plums
To the Nines
Ten Big Ones

Coming Soon
Smitten

JANET EVANOVICH

Love Overboard

(Originally published as *Ivan Takes a Wife*)

HarperTorch
An Imprint of HarperCollinsPublishers

This book was originally published as a *Loveswept* paperback in 1989, in a slightly altered form, as *Ivan Takes a Wife*, by Bantam Books, a division of Bantam Doubleday Dell Publishing Group, Inc.

This is a work of fiction. Names, characters, places, and incidents are products of the author's imagination or are used fictitiously and are not to be construed as real. Any resemblance to actual events, locales, organizations, or persons, living or dead, is entirely coincidental.

HARPERTORCH
An Imprint of HarperCollins*Publishers*
10 East 53rd Street
New York, New York 10022-5299

Copyright © 1989, 2005 by Janet Evanovich
Excerpt from *Back to the Bedroom* copyright © 1989, 2005 by Janet Evanovich
Author photo by Deborah Feingold
ISBN: 0-06-113721-9

First HarperTorch special printing: June 2006
First HarperTorch paperback printing: February 2005

HarperCollins®, HarperTorch™, and ❦™ are trademarks of HarperCollins Publishers Inc.

Printed in the United States of America

Visit HarperTorch on the World Wide Web at www.harpercollins.com

10 9 8 7 6 5 4 3

*To Alex—my adventuress
who walks to the beat
of her own drum.*

Chapter 1

Ivan Rasmussen swirled the last of his coffee around the bottom of his mug, looked past the prow of his ship to the sloping green lawn of Camden Harbor Park, and wondered for the hundredth time in the past two hours what the devil had happened to his cook, Lucy. She was *never* late. Until now. Now she was beyond late, and because she was his friend as well as his cook, he was worried.

He squinted at a flash of color and movement toward the top of the hill, and unconsciously let his mouth fall open at the sight of a young woman rolling down the grass embankment. She came to a spread-eagled stop when she reached the cement footpath at the bottom, and she uttered an expletive that carried across the short span of shoreline, bringing the first smile of the day to Ivan's lips.

1

Stephanie Lowe, the woman Ivan had been watching, struggled to her feet, adjusted her battered backpack, and scowled at the grass stains on her knees. She was looking ahead to a whole week of cooking for Ivan the Terrible in exchange for free plumbing repairs to her bathroom. And if that wasn't awful enough, she was the one who had to bring Ivan the good news that his usual cook was taking an impromptu vacation.

"Lord, I'm such a *dope!*" Stephanie muttered, smacking herself on the forehead, broadcasting her thoughts to all watching. Nothing like making a memorable entrance. If one more thing went wrong, she was going home. The heck with it all, she thought. She wasn't crazy about this deal anyway. She'd seen Ivan only once, but he'd made a lasting impression on her. He was over six feet with gray-green eyes and strawberry blond hair. And at the time of their meeting he'd been all packaged up in a custom-tailored, navy pin-striped suit that had made him look more like a chairman of the board than the captain of a schooner.

Stephanie searched the crowded harbor for the *Josiah T. Savage*, gasping when she realized it was directly in front of her, tied to a floating dock at the end of the cement path. It would be the last of the windjammers to leave the harbor, she thought with an inward groan—late to leave Camden because it was waiting for its cook. Unfortunately, its cook had suddenly decided to get married. Double unfortunately, its cook was her cousin Lucy.

Lucy had provided her with a few vital statistics on the *Savage.* It was a windship. A tall ship. A hundred-year-old, two-masted, coasting schooner with seventy feet of deck length, carrying twenty-two passengers and four crew members on six-day cruises along the island-strewn coast of Maine. Lucy's description of her captain had been equally brief. Ivan Rasmussen, she'd said, was better known as Ivan the Terrible because he was terribly handsome, terribly eligible, and terribly slippery. Stephanie had her own reasons for believing he was terribly rotten.

She took a quick survey of the ship and spotted Ivan standing on deck, coffee mug in hand, looking at her as if she'd just dropped off the planet Mars.

Get it together, Stephanie, she told herself. Life was filled with trade-offs. If you packed away a whole bag of cookies, then you had to wash them down with diet root beer. This was just another of life's cans of diet root beer. Cousin Lucy worked as a cook on Ivan's windjammer. That morning cousin Lucy had decided to run off and marry Stanley Shelton. Stanley Shelton was a plumber. Stephanie desperately needed a plumber. Simple, right? Cousin Lucy got a honeymoon, and Stephanie got a toilet. Okay, no problem. Piece of cake. There was no reason to be nervous. Ivan should be happy to have her aboard, she reasoned. Where else would he get a cook on such short notice? She was actually doing him a favor.

Besides, after what he'd done to her, he deserved to eat her cooking for a week. Anyway, how hard could it be? She'd just whip up forty or fifty peanut butter and jelly sandwiches and send all the passengers off to an island in the dinghy. It might even be fun—a week on the high seas with the wind at her back and the salt spray in her face. It was going to be an adventure. A new experience.

She approached the boarding ramp and looked up into Ivan's eyes, deciding they seemed only mildly predatory, more curious than anything else, narrowed against the glare, shaded by thick curly blond lashes. His hair was longer and lighter than Stephanie had re-membered it, curling over his ears and along the nape of his neck. He'd grown a beard since she'd seen him—very close-cropped, oddly dark compared to his hair, and overwhelm-ingly masculine. He wore faded, frayed cutoff jeans that Stephanie admitted were perfectly proper but seemed sinfully erotic, molded to Ivan's male contours.

She bridged the short span between wharf and ship, automatically taking inventory of her surroundings, and plastered a hopeful smile on her lips. "Hello."

"Hello," he responded, contained amuse-ment clear in his voice.

There was a flicker of recognition in his eyes, but Stephanie knew he hadn't placed her. She wasn't surprised. He probably swindled women all the time. He probably couldn't keep track of all the people he'd stuck it to. "Stephanie Lowe," she said. "We met two months ago when I bought your house." The very same house that had been falling apart piece by piece ever since she'd moved in, she silently added.

Ivan's brows drew together. Stephanie Lowe, his cook's cousin, the woman who'd bought Haben. How could he have forgotten Stephanie Lowe? Early Alzheimer's disease, he decided. He was suffering from premature senile dementia. He'd seen Stephanie Lowe only briefly at the Realtor's office, but he should have remembered. She'd worn a SpongeBob T-shirt, and she'd been disappointed to find he didn't own a parrot.

She was just as outrageous now as before, he thought. Her hair was short and shiny brown with wispy bangs. It would have been pretty if it hadn't been sticking out in all directions. He supposed she was one of those punk people. He did a mental calculation and put her at five-foot-seven, noticing she was slim and long-legged, wearing chunky silver, green, and white high-tops, bright pink socks scrunched down around her ankles, a pair of rumpled khaki walking shorts, and an orange tank top that was bright enough to get them through the best fogbank Maine could muster. She was probably there to complain about the house. Just what he needed to round out his morning. "Lucy tells me you've been having some problems with the house . . ."

"Problems?" Stephanie felt her control slipping. It wasn't her strong suit to begin with.

"Two weeks after I moved in, the front porch rotted out from under me. Then the water heater blew up and flooded the cellar. None of the windows will open, and it's hotter than heck in—" She stopped when she saw the smile spread across his face. "Something funny about a water heater exploding?"

Ivan didn't think there was anything funny about a water heater exploding, and he couldn't understand how so many things could go wrong with his house. He'd left it in perfect condition. He loved Haben. It had belonged to his family for generations, and he would never have sold it if it hadn't been absolutely necessary. He was smiling despite everything because Stephanie Lowe was a sight that inspired smiles.

"I think you're cute when you get all steamed up," he admitted, and playfully patted her cowlick. "Why is your hair sticking up? Is this a new style?"

Stephanie felt the top of her head. "When the upstairs toilet broke, it leaked onto the floor and collapsed the ceiling in the kitchen and downstairs bathroom. When the ceiling fell down in the bathroom, it took the mirrored door off the medicine chest and smashed it on

7

the sink. Since that was the only mirror in the house, I had to comb my hair in front of the toaster."

Ivan stared at her. Maybe she was wacko and was making all this up. No, chances were good that she was wacko, but she wasn't making it up. Lucy had told him about the porch and the water heater, and Stephanie's hair *did* look as though it had been combed in front of a toaster.

"I'm really sorry," he said. "I honestly thought the house was in good shape when I sold it."

Stephanie bit back a rude word. It wouldn't pay to get vulgar. If she wanted her toilet fixed, she was going to have to spend a week with this rip-off Romeo.

"Actually, the condition of the house sort of explains why I'm here. You see, I hadn't planned on all these disasters. I'd intended to turn the house into a bed-and-breakfast inn, and the plain truth is that until I get some paying customers, I'm going to have a cash flow problem. So when Lucy showed up this morning and told me she was getting married . . ."

Ivan looked pained. "Lucy, my cook, is getting married? Does this have something to do with her being late?"

"Bingo."

Pieces of the puzzle fell together in his mind. "And does this have something to do with your being here wearing a backpack?"

"Right again. You see, Lucy's marrying a plumber . . ."

Ivan groaned. "I've got it figured out. Can you cook?"

"Of course I can cook."

"For twenty-six people?"

"No sweat. Just point me to the microwave."

The grin returned to Ivan's mouth, and the corners of his eyes crinkled. At least Lucy had sent him someone with a sense of humor.

Stephanie's pack slipped, and Ivan reached to get it, his hand momentarily trapped between the padded strap and the smooth, warm skin of her bare shoulder. He took a moment to enjoy the feeling and wondered what it would be like to kiss her. She had a very kissable mouth, he decided. Soft and feminine, perfectly shaped. Her eyes were blue and wary, shaded by a fringe of black lash and topped with eyebrows that looked like bird wings. The flush on her cheeks told him she was also feeling some attraction, and the set to her chin told him she had no intention of succumbing to it.

Just as well, he thought, hefting the pack onto his own shoulder. She was sort of an employee, and he made it a rule never to mix business and pleasure. Of course, he was the direct descendant of a famous pirate, and as such he was supposed to break a few rules now and then. He motioned toward the forward hatch. "I'll show you to your quarters. Watch your head and always go down the ladder backward."

Stephanie followed him belowdecks and found herself in a fairly large room that held the shape of the prow of the ship. Polished oak banquettes lined the walls and were spanned by a massive triangular table. Brass lanterns swung from the ceiling just as they must have a hundred years ago. A copper jug filled with wildflowers sat in the middle of the table, and red-and-white-checkered curtains fluttered from open windows.

"Breakfast and supper are usually eaten here," Ivan said. "Weather permitting, we eat lunch topside." He pointed to the back corner of the room. "This is the galley."

Stephanie nodded, taking in the small sink, oak counter, black iron woodstove across from the sink, the spice racks lining the wall, pots, pans, utensils, and sprays of dried herbs hanging overhead. "Very cozy," she said. "Where's the kitchen?"

"The galley *is* the kitchen."

Stephanie felt her heart stop. He had to be kidding. "Yes, but where's the stove? Where's the refrigerator? Where's the food processor?"

Ivan's mouth tightened a fraction of an inch. "*This* is the stove," he said, pulling Stephanie into the tiny galley. "This is all we've got. Have you ever cooked on a woodstove?"

Who did she look like, Annie Oakley? Of course she'd never cooked on a woodstove. Until two months ago she'd lived in Jersey City. People didn't cook on woodstoves in Jersey City. At least, not the people she knew. Most of the people she knew didn't cook at all. She guessed that wasn't the answer he wanted to hear, so she decided to lie. "Don't worry," she said, "woodstove is my middle name."

Dollars to doughnuts she can't boil water, Ivan thought. At least she had the guts to lie. He was thankful for that. It was a start.

"I have to go up to cast off. We're already late getting out of the harbor." He gestured to a short red curtain over one of the banquettes. "That's your bunk. You can get settled in, and

I'll be back as soon as I can get free. Keep the coffee going, and you'll probably want to take inventory of the food Lucy's stored in for the week."

What she really wanted to do was put her hands around Lucy's neck and squeeze. "Don't worry about me. I'll be fine down here . . . taking inventory."

She took the backpack from Ivan and went over to check out the red curtain. Behind the curtain was a narrow bunk built into the wooden wall of the ship. It was nicely made up in crisp white sheets and a red plaid woolen blanket. Lucy's belongings were neatly packed away in a small storage area over the bunk. Fortunately, she and Lucy were the same size, and it would be possible to supplement her meager wardrobe with Lucy's meager wardrobe.

Stephanie went back to the stove and peered into the two blue enamel coffeepots. They were full to the brim and steaming hot, and the combined aroma of woodstove and fresh coffee almost knocked her to her knees.

She didn't know what she'd expected, but it wasn't this. She'd expected the Love Boat, maybe. Something slick and touristy. This was slick in a good way, she decided. There was a feeling of solid reality to it. It was immaculately clean, carefully restored, and everywhere she looked there was quality. It was impossible not to get caught up in the magic of the ship. Not only did she feel transported back in time, but she was overwhelmed by the atmosphere of warmth and well-being that filled every space of the forward cabin.

She took a wad of folded papers from her pocket and smoothed them out on the counter. While she'd been packing and Stanley had been checking out the toilet, Lucy had frantically prepared a detailed six-day schedule.

"Okay, everything I need to know to be an A-one ship's cook," Stephanie said. She narrowed her eyes at the menu. According to Lucy, she was supposed to begin by making yeast rolls for supper and fish stew, biscuits, chocolate chip cookies, and fresh fruit for lunch. Stephanie checked her watch. Eleven o'clock. She looked at the woodstove and thought authenticity had been carried a bit far.

Ivan squatted at the top of the ladder. "How's it going?"

"We're stopping at a fast-food place for lunch, aren't we?"

13

He grimaced and left.

"Does that mean *no*?" Stephanie called after him.

A young man swung down the stairs Tarzan style. His T-shirt was three sizes too large, and his baggy shorts hung precariously low on his hips. He struck a negligent pose against the stairwell and looked at her over the top of his dark glasses.

"Ace," he said with a crooked grin. "I'm here to answer your every need."

Ivan reappeared. "He's here to do your dishes and peel your potatoes. He's nineteen and walking on very thin ice." He gave Ace a stern look and vanished.

"The captain runs a tight ship," Ace explained. "And I'm kind of a loose sort of guy."

"You know anything about working this woodstove?"

"Sure."

"Good. You're in charge. I do the cooking, and you do the wood stuff."

Ace took a chunk of wood from the cache under the stove and flipped it into the air. He spun around and caught the wood one-handed. "I'm good with my hands," he said, giving Stephanie another crooked grin.

This poor kid has watched too many Tom Cruise movies, Stephanie thought. He had him down pretty well, too, except Ace's nose was larger, making him seem closer to Snoopy doing Joe Cool.

"Okay, Ace, I'm going to give your hands a chance to make lunch. I think we'll have an abbreviated menu of fish chowder and biscuits. I don't suppose we have twenty or thirty cans of fish chowder lying around somewhere?"

"Don't suppose we do."

"Okay," Stephanie said, "then we'll go to plan two. Find a recipe for the blasted stuff." She fumbled in the cabinet drawer for Lucy's recipe book and tore out the chowder page. "You assemble the soup ingredients, and I'll get started on the biscuits." Her eyes opened wide at the biscuit recipe. "Twelve cups of flour? I'll need a cement mixer to make this recipe."

Ace plunked a huge earthenware bowl onto the counter and gave Stephanie's waist a squeeze. "This is the bowl Lucy uses for biscuits," he said, dropping a kiss on Stephanie's shoulder.

Stephanie waved a large wooden spoon at him. "This is the spoon Stephanie uses for smacking knuckles. Kiss me again, and you'll never play the piano."

Ace looked insulted. "How can you resist me? I'm a cool dude."

"Listen, Ace, I'm going to level with you. I don't know diddly about cooking for twenty-six people, I've never been on a ship before, and this is the first time I've seen a woodstove up close. I'm doing this so my cousin Lucy can have a honeymoon, and—"

"Lucy got married? No joke?"

"She's marrying Stanley Shelton, the plumber."

Ace looked impressed. "It's always nice to have a plumber in the family."

"My sentiments exactly."

He took a cauldron from a ceiling hook and set it on the stove. "Lucy's a real good guy, and any cousin of Lucy's is a cousin of mine. I'm gonna help you out here."

An ally! Stephanie felt weak with relief, but there was one more thing she had to find out. "Can I ask you a question? Isn't it hard to see in here with those dark glasses on? You aren't doing drugs, are you?"

"Not me. I'm too cool to do drugs. I'd take these glasses off, but I'm getting glare from your socks." He gave Stephanie a meaningful look. "So you think it's going to work out between us?"

"Yup. I think we're going to be a great kitchen team."

"Mmm. And what about romance?" He pointed to the bunk on the opposite side of the table. "We're roomies, you know."

"Sorry, romance is out of the question. I'm not into romance. You're very tempting, but I took a vow."

He pulled some onions out of a vegetable bin behind the ladder. "This is going to ruin my image. And my self-esteem is shot to hell."

"Life is cruel," Stephanie said, counting out twelve cups of flour. She looked around the small galley. "Where's the butter?"

"Ice chest's on deck."

She wiped her hands on her shorts and gave him a thumbs-up sign, deciding he was a good guy—a little weird, maybe, but not mean.

She went topside and discovered they were almost out of Camden Harbor. She'd watched the schooners come and go over the past two months, usually from an upstairs window or from the widow's walk on the top of her house. The big wooden boats were eerily quiet for their size. Not having the power of an inboard motor, Ivan relied on a yawl to move them through the flotilla of pleasure craft into open sea, where the sails could be unfurled.

The rigging creaked and clanked in the breeze, and the town of Camden looked very small, hugging the waterline, the steeple of the Chestnut Street Baptist Church sparkling in the morning sun. From this distance the mountains seemed to push against the town's back. Wisps of fog caught in the treetops on Mt. Battie, and Stephanie could see patches of yellow, orange, and red, where autumn leaves had already begun to turn. A gull rode a clanging buoy, oblivious to the noise. Passengers sat topside, watching the gull, watching Ivan at the helm, waiting for the sails to go up. And in an hour they'll be waiting for lunch, Stephanie thought with a groan.

Ace smiled at her when she returned to the galley with the butter. "I was afraid you'd gone overboard."

"No. Just took a minute to enjoy the scenery." She peeked into the steaming brew on the stove. "What is this?"

"Lucy's fish chowder. I followed her recipe, but I think she must have left something out. Do you think it smells funny?"

It had passed smelling funny, Stephanie decided. It was more in the category of frightening. "What are those little round things floating on top?"

Ace stared into the pot. "They look like fish eyes."

"Omigod."

"You think I should have cut off the heads before I put the fish in the hot water?"

Stephanie clapped her hand over her mouth to squelch the laughter. She composed herself as best she could. "Nah, why waste a perfectly good fish head? This will be fine. We'll . . . um, strain it before we serve it."

"We might not have to do that," Ace said. "Most of the folks on this cruise are pretty old. They probably can't see so good. We could tell them they're beans or something."

Ivan came halfway down the ladder and stopped in midstride, immediately backing up a step. "What are you cooking down here, rubber boots? It smells like the fish-processing plant in Rockland on a bad day."

"You think you can do better?"

He was sure he couldn't do any worse. "I'm not really an expert at this," he said gently, "but I think if you reduced the heat somehow, so it wasn't boiling so furiously . . ." He held his breath and hoped the fumes wouldn't peel the varnish off the walls.

"I think you're right." Stephanie gave the pot a clonk with her wooden spoon. "We're going to reduce the heat right away." She looked at Ace. "How about turning down the wood?"

Ace stared at her, his eyes hidden behind the silver-black lenses. "That's the problem. You see, the wood control dial is broken."

Stephanie looked at Ivan. "The wood control dial is broken," she repeated with an absolutely straight face.

Ivan nodded. "Well, that explains it." He inched his way back up the ladder, wondering what he'd done to deserve this. He'd cheated on his U.S. history exam in seventh grade, he'd wheedled Mary Ann Kulecza out of her panties in eighth grade, and he'd padded charitable contributions on his income tax. Now it was all coming home to roost. God had sent him Stephanie Lowe.

"After you turn the wood down, you should probably try to snag some eyes," Stephanie told Ace.

"That's going to be tough. They're hidden under all this scum."

An hour later the ship was heading due east, pitching through open seas. The scum had been ladled off, and the fish eyes slopped in the broth, mercilessly bashing themselves against the side of the big metal pot while Ace hunted them down with his spoon. Sweat rolled in rivulets along Stephanie's back and collected on her upper lip as she stood guard over her baking biscuits.

"Any problems?" Ivan called down. "Folks are getting hungry."

"Tell them to keep their pants on. You can't rush a gourmet feast like this," Stephanie yelled over the sizzle of coffee splattering on the hot stove. She opened the oven door, whipped out a tray of biscuits, and dumped them in a bread basket lined with a red linen napkin. "Hardly burned at all," she told Ace. "I don't think we even have to scrape the black off the bottoms of this batch."

Ace took time out of his fish-eye hunt to appreciate the biscuits.

"How many eyes have you got?" Stephanie asked.

Ace poked around in the cup sitting next to the stove. "Seven. Looks like I'm only missing one. You think we could have had a one-eyed fish?"

"You keep looking while I take the biscuits up." She assembled a tray of chowder mugs, soup spoons, napkins, and tubs of butter, and set them on the roof of the midship cabin. She added baskets of biscuits and bowls of fresh fruit, and felt her lip curl involuntarily when Ace appeared with the tureen of fish stew.

"Are you going to eat this?" he asked in a whisper.

Eat it? Was he kidding? She'd inhaled enough fish stew to last her a lifetime.

Mrs. Pease got a peculiar expression on her face halfway through her lunch. She was short and round with dimpled elbows and dimpled knees and short curly white hair. She slid her glasses low on her nose and squinted into her soup. "There's something staring at me in here."

Her husband looked over her shoulder. "I don't see anything."

"Right there." She pointed with her spoon. "It's a little bitty eyeball."

"That's ridiculous," he said. "What would an eyeball be doing in your soup?"

Ace jumped to Mrs. Pease's side and dipped his spoon into her mug. "Okay, where is it? Where's this eyeball from outer space?" He held the spoon an inch from his nose and studied its contents. "That's not an eyeball. That's a black-eyed pea." He fired the object off his spoon slingshot style, and a seagull caught it in midair. "Seagulls love black-eyed peas," he told Mrs. Pease. He looked at Stephanie and mouthed the word "eight."

Stephanie took a biscuit and avoided looking in Ivan's direction.

"Our captain is staring," Ace said. "You think he knows it was an eyeball?"

"Not a chance."

"He looks intense," Ace said. "I've only seen him look like that one time before. It was when Andy Newfarmer's dog lifted his leg on Ivan's new all-weather boots, and Ivan was in them."

Stephanie nibbled on the biscuit. "What's Ivan like? Have you known him long?"

"Ivan's first-class. Comes from an old seafaring family. His grandfather and great-grandfather were captains of coasting schooners, and people tell me Ivan's a descendant of Red Rasmussen, the pirate. Supposedly, Ivan's house, Haben, is haunted by the ghost of Red's widow. Lucy said Ivan sold the house this summer."

Great, Stephanie thought, I bought a haunted

house. Another point of interest the real estate lady failed to mention.

A gust of wind rattled the sails, Ivan spun the wheel, the ship leaned into the wind and surged ahead, and Stephanie found herself watching Ivan, trying to sort through a mixture of uncomfortable emotions. As much as she hated to admit it, he was awesome. He stood in calm control with a suggestion of suppressed power in his wide stance and steady hand. His beard hugged the angle of his jaw, making him look like the perfect captain for a ship named *Savage*. He was a man who felt comfortable with authority and inspired confidence. An hour ago she wouldn't have trusted him to change the kitty litter, and now she was trapped on a little wooden boat, bobbing around in a huge ocean, counting on Ivan to keep her safe. And she was sure he would. Stephanie thought he looked very fierce and wondered if he could also be gentle.

Their gazes locked, and Stephanie felt her face flame. She'd been caught gawking. Actually, gawking wasn't accurate. Drooling was closer to the truth. Cousin Lucy hadn't been kidding when she'd said Ivan was terribly attractive.

Stephanie's heart skipped a beat when she saw him hand the wheel over to the first mate and turn in her direction. Okay, she thought, if he criticizes the soup, I'll apologize. And if he kissed her, she'd drag him down to the galley. The last thought produced a mental grimace. Good grief! Get a grip, she told herself.

Chapter 2

There was no doubt in Ivan's mind that there had been a fish eye in Mrs. Pease's chowder. He was equally sure that he didn't want to know how the fish eye had gotten there. There were some things best left untouched. And there were some things that were mystical in nature—such as why he was so attracted to Stephanie Lowe, a woman who apparently lived side by side with catastrophe. Maybe it wasn't attraction. Maybe it was simply gruesome fascination. The sort of grim curiosity that compels you to stare at bloody victims of auto accidents and read about serial killers in the newspaper.

Now that he knew Stephanie better, he wasn't at all surprised her house was falling apart. And if she stayed aboard the *Savage*, there was no telling what would happen. The plague would strike, or they'd run aground. At the very least, she'd poison them all. Stephanie Lowe was an accident just waiting to happen.

Too bad she was going to have to go, he thought as he approached her. There was an energy about her that was entertaining, and she was terrific-looking, in an unconventional sort of way. She had a few freckles across her straight little nose, silky smooth skin, and big blue eyes that were, at the moment, turning his stomach upside down. Her body language said "back off," but there was something about the expression in those cobalt eyes that made his jeans fit tighter than usual. Not that it mattered. He wasn't a man who took a casual view of sex, and he wasn't the sort of man who let the fit of his jeans influence business decisions. His intuition told him to put her off on the first island, but he knew he'd have to keep her on board until he found a replacement. A Calamity Jane cook was better than no cook at all.

He took an apple from the bowl behind Stephanie and held it in his hand, enjoying the confrontation. She was waiting for him to make the first move, and her eyes weren't giving away anything. She wasn't going to initiate a conversation about her cooking, and she wasn't going to flirt with him. It was a damn shame she couldn't cook. And it was an even worse shame she wasn't going to flirt.

He smiled at her, hoping she'd smile back. He liked her better when she was more at ease, muttering curse words and rolling down hills. When she returned the smile, he offered her the apple. "Have you had a chance to investigate the ship?"

She shook her head. "I've only gone as far as the galley and the ice chest."

"Why don't you take a few minutes off, and I'll give you a quick tour while Ace handles cleanup."

He started at the midship deckhouse. "We have two heads. They have flush toilets, hot and cold running water, and they're both above deck." He opened a door and revealed a clean lavatory. He latched the lavatory door from the outside and pointed to the hatch just opposite it. "That leads to the midship cabin with accommodations for twelve passengers." He motioned to the structure directly in front of him. "This is the aft deckhouse."

Stephanie followed him around the aft deckhouse and down the ship's ladder to a small room with a scarred wooden gaming table and bench seats, big enough for four people. Three double cabins were located off the left side of the room. A small delft blue-and-white-tiled, brass-fitted fireplace had been built into the far corner, behind the table. Bookshelves lined all the available wall space, and a brass ship's lantern hung from the ceiling. It was a room that invited you to stay for a game of checkers, and almost made you wish for a dark, drizzly day so you could huddle at the table with a mug of tea, the fire at your back, and a good book in hand.

Ivan opened the only door on the right side and motioned Stephanie in. "This is my cabin." He had a double bunk and a window at eye level, similar to the passengers' cabins, but his quarters also included a compact sitting room with a built-in desk, racks for maps, and a wall full of navigational equipment.

"This vessel is Coast Guard approved with radar and marine radio," he said. "We have a small crew, and I like everyone to have at least a basic understanding of this equipment." No matter how short their stay, he silently added.

Stephanie looked at the switches and dials and found them to be far less intimidating than the woodstove. She was momentarily diverted by the wind rattling in the sails. There was a lull, then the ship heeled to as it changed direction, knocking her off-balance in the narrow quarters, flinging her at Ivan. She heard his breath hitch in his throat as her breasts flattened against his chest, and her leg accidentally snaked between his.

"Whoops!" Stephanie said, grasping Ivan by the shirtfront. "Guess I don't have my sea legs yet."

His hands clasped her waist, and Stephanie felt as if the air had suddenly become too thick to breathe. He was warm and firm, and she had an overwhelming desire to explore the contour of his shoulder and let her fingers travel the length of his back. She watched his eyes focus on her mouth and knew he was going to kiss her.

"This probably isn't such a good idea . . ." Stephanie murmured without much conviction.

"It's a damn stupid idea," he answered, his hands possessively tightening on her hips as he dragged her closer. His mouth moved over hers, and they clung to each other in an exchange of passion that was far too powerful, too intimate, too perfect to have happened be-

31

tween strangers. They paused and watched each other warily, trying to assess what had just taken place.

Sun-bleached eyebrows drew together over Ivan's eyes as he wrestled with his sense of propriety. If he didn't stop kissing her right then, nature would definitely follow its course. It was not the sort of initiation he ordinarily gave his new crew members and certainly not the way he preferred to start a cruise. Not to mention, cabin walls were a quarter inch thick, and this was the woman who had rolled down the hill and uttered an expletive that carried halfway across Camden Harbor. Lord knows what she'd be like in the throes of passion. She could be a screamer or a groaner!

He clenched his teeth, took her by the shoulders, and positioned her against the wall. "Stay right there! Don't sway, don't jiggle, don't breathe heavy."

Stephanie pressed herself into the paneling and struggled to gain some control, noticing that Ivan wasn't doing too well at regulating his breathing either. "Wow," she said.

Ivan nodded in mute agreement, keeping his gaze on the floor while he wondered just how fast he could find another cook if he really put his mind to it. He was going to have to wear a midthigh raincoat for the rest of the trip if he didn't get rid of Stephanie Lowe.

"I don't think this is going to work out," he finally said. "I think it would be best if I radio around and try to find another cook."

"You can't do that! I need a toilet!" Stephanie narrowed her eyes. "Boy, you have a lot of nerve. First you foist your ramshackle house off on me. Then you practically attack me and use it as an excuse to kick me off the ship. I'm going to get the Better Business Bureau after you. I'm going to call the League of Women Voters. I'm going to tell your mother!"

Ivan ran his hand through his hair. "First of all, my house wasn't ramshackle until you moved in. Second, that was a mutual attack. Third . . ." He stopped and sighed. Stephanie's big blue eyes were shining with fury, and her lips were pressed tightly together in indignation. She didn't like this any more than he did, he thought, but she really needed Stanley Shelton to fix her plumbing. He swore softly, knowing he wouldn't try to get another cook, and plucked a piece of leaf from her hair. "You picked up some hitchhikers when you tripped and rolled down the hill," he said, his smile returning.

Stephanie combed her hair with her fingers, looking for more leaves. "I didn't trip. I was pushed."

Ivan looked at her sideways. "I don't remember seeing anyone else up there."

"I know. Isn't that odd? I was sure I was alone, and then all of a sudden I felt two hands give me a shove."

"Anyone ever tell you that you're very strange?"

"Yeah, well, strange things have been happening to me ever since I bought your house. I had a perfectly normal life till then."

Ivan nudged her out the door. "I find it hard to believe you ever had a normal life. What did you do before you became an innkeeper?"

"You're pretty nosy."

Ivan snagged her by the back of her shirt as she started up the ladder. "I have a right to know my employees' work records."

She couldn't argue with that, but she wasn't ready to talk about her previous job. And besides, she was annoyed that he had figured she wasn't normal. She turned to face him. "I was sort of a teacher, sometimes . . . in a government program." And this wasn't the first time she'd had to hedge about her work. Go ahead, ask her anything. She was a master at evasion.

He looked skeptical. "Why did you stop teaching? You get fired for wearing illegal socks? Accidentally misplace some of your students?"

Stephanie shrugged. "I just got tired of it. I decided it was time to get away." Time to get away before she was blown away, she thought ruefully. She wasn't effective anymore. In three months she'd be thirty. Too old to fit in with teens. Too well known for her own good. And her personal life was a shambles.

"My whole family is in Jersey City. All the kids I went to high school with are still in Jersey City. Do you know, every Sunday for the past eight years I've gone to my parents' house for roast chicken dinner. Think about it . . . eight years of roast chicken. Four hundred and sixteen chickens!"

"That's a lot of chicken."

"I love all those people, but I need something new. I guess I need to find myself. Pretty corny, huh?" She shook her head in amazement. "My work was so consuming, I took the easy way out on personal relationships. I needed them to be safe and predictable, and so

I was calmly going around and around and around in circles. I'd made these daily grooves that I was able to follow without even thinking. One day Steve, the guy I'd been dating for four years, told me he had this special announcement. I thought he was going to propose to me. Turned out he was going to officially marry his roommate Roger." She rolled her eyes. "All those years I thought Steve was shy! I kept wondering why he wasn't interested in . . . uh, well, anyway, that was why we never got around to . . ."

"Wait a minute. You went with a guy for four years and you never . . . and then it turned out he was gay?"

"Well, I wouldn't have anyway. I'm saving myself for marriage."

Swell. A virgin. He had his stomach tied in knots for the only virgin left on the East Coast. "Lady, you're not going to keep your virgin status very long if you go around kissing heterosexuals like you kissed me a minute ago." He leaned his back on the wood-paneled wall and loosely crossed his arms over his chest. "I think it's safe to say your chances of keeping it until you're married are slim. Especially if you stay on this ship."

Stephanie slumped against the ladder. "You have a point. Twenty seconds ago I didn't give a hoot about my virginity. It was a lot easier to have high standards when I was dating Steve." Stephanie made a flamboyant gesture with her hands. "I should have seen what was happening. I should have realized there was something wrong with our relationship, but I'd gotten so dull, so placid when I wasn't working. I had to have a comfortable personal routine because I didn't have any energy left over for myself. Boy, was I boring, or what? It's no wonder Steve dumped me for Roger."

Ivan grinned. He couldn't imagine her being boring. She was bright and sexy and talked faster than any two people put together.

Stephanie grimaced at the painful memory of rejection. She'd said too much, but once she'd gotten started, it had all poured out. Not that it mattered. The only thing significant about her personal life was that it was insignificant. "Anyway, I decided to start over. So I cleaned out my paltry savings account and went to Atlantic City to gamble."

"And you made a big killing?"

"No. My uncle Ed died while I was there and

left me all his money. That's how I bought your house . . . with Uncle Ed's money."

It had seemed like the perfect move. It was the antithesis of her former life. It was calm, cozy, *normal.* It would give her a chance to meet people who weren't staring back at her down the snub-nosed barrel of her service revolver.

She turned, pulled herself halfway up the ladder, and stopped. She looked at Ivan over her shoulder. "Is the house really haunted?"

"Some people think so."

"Do you?"

He put a friendly hand on her backside and encouraged her to go topside. "I think you'd better check on Ace. Make sure he doesn't knead anything other than bread dough. He's hell on divorced women, and we have three of them on this cruise."

Stephanie scooted up the ladder and blinked in the bright sunshine. "You avoided my original question."

"Does it bother you that the house might be haunted?"

She paused at the hatch to the galley. "I don't know. I guess it would depend on who was haunting it. And you still haven't answered my question."

"There's a very fine line between imagination and reality when it comes to things like ghosts. I think it's just a matter of what you choose to believe."

"So what you're telling me is that my house is haunted."

"Definitely. But don't worry about it. It's only my aunt Tess. She's an old lady."

"How old?"

"About three hundred years. She's hardly noticeable. She prowls the widow's walk in the fog, and sometimes she sits on the window seat in the master bedroom." He waved his hand in a dismissive gesture when he saw the look of horror on her face. "Actually, she hardly ever sits on the window seat. Once or twice a year, maybe."

"She hates me," Stephanie said.

"What?"

"She's undoubtedly the one who pushed me down the hill."

"Aunt Tess wouldn't do a thing like that."

"Oh! A lot you know about your aunt Tess. Suddenly it all makes perfect sense. The woman is vicious! She probably broke my toilet. I'd bet money on it."

"Ghosts don't go around breaking toilets.

39

They moan and drag chains and walk through walls."

"Then how else would you explain my house problems?"

"If you're trying to get me to admit to negligence, it isn't working. It's an old house, and things break. Although I have to admit it *is* strange. That porch was in good condition when I moved out. Wood just doesn't rot that fast. Tell you what, as soon as we get back to Camden, I'll have a talk with Aunt Tess. See if I can calm her down."

Stephanie gave him a black look. "You're just humoring me. You don't really think she broke my toilet, do you?"

The grin widened. "She was the wife of a pirate. She could be capable of anything."

"You think I need Ghostbusters?"

"I think you need to go below and make sure Ace doesn't have a woman stowed in his bunk."

An hour later Stephanie was up to her elbows in chocolate chip cookie batter. "You mean to tell me Lucy bakes cookies like this every day?"

Ace picked a handful of chocolate morsels

out of the huge bowl and popped them into his mouth.

"Yup. She gets up about five and starts the stove. By six o'clock she's made hot coffee, and she starts chucking trays of cookies in. Lucy just keeps the cookies going all day while she bakes other stuff. Usually she makes the dough the night before."

Stephanie dropped a glob of dough onto a cookie sheet. "Don't these poor people ever get any *real* cookies? You know, like Oreos and Fig Newtons?"

"Nope. We force them to eat homemade," Ace said, reaching for more chocolate.

Stephanie opened the oven door and felt her mind go momentarily slack at the sight of wall-to-wall ham. Hot air rushed out at her, carrying the spicy smell of cloves and Lucy's special honey glaze. There was just enough room at the top for one tray of cookies, so she slid it in.

Stephanie closed the door on the ham and cookies and threw a skeptical glance at Ace. "You think this is going to work?"

"Sure. Just watch the little temperature gauge on the front of the stove."

Stephanie squinted at the gauge. Five hundred degrees. You could probably bake a brick at that temperature, she thought. She stared at the stove for five minutes, then opened the door and took out a tray of charred cookies. "How do we get this sucker cooled off? Fast."

Ace pulled a stack of paper shopping bags from a cubbyhole under the sink. "Lucy wets these and puts them in the oven. She says it brings the temperature down."

Stephanie soaked the bags and stuffed them in around the ham. She added another tray of cookies, closed the door, and secretly tried to bribe God into lowering the heat. If you just do this one thing for me, she promised, I'll never say another curseword, I'll eat all my vegetables, I'll drive at the speed limit.

Mr. and Mrs. Pease carefully lowered themselves down the fo'c'sle stairs. "Isn't this cozy?" Mrs. Pease said. "And it smells wonderful down here."

Mr. Pease poured two mugs of coffee and peered into the bowl of cookie dough. "Did you use oat flour?" he asked Stephanie.

"Nope. Just plain old flour flour."

He shook his head. "Oat flour's the secret to a chewy cookie. You have to use some oat flour, and you can't bake them too long."

Mrs. Pease took a mug from her husband.

"He's a wonderful cookie baker," she told Stephanie. "You'd never know they were homemade."

Stephanie sniffed and rubbed her eyes. "Is it always this smoky in here?" she asked Ace.

"Smoky?" Ace removed his dark glasses. "You're right. It's smoky." He checked the flue and shook his head. "I don't know what's wrong. The flue is okay."

"Maybe something's burning in the oven," Mrs. Pease suggested.

Stephanie opened the door and jumped back as a wall of smoke and flame rolled out at her.

"Jeez," Ace said, "looks like the bags caught fire. That never happened when Lucy did it."

Stephanie stuck her hand into a thick potholder mitt, pulled the flaming bags out of the oven, and hurled them into the sink.

Mrs. Pease put her hand to her heart. "We're gonna die. The ship's gonna burn to a cinder, and we're gonna drown."

Stephanie fanned the air with a hand towel. "This is how we lower the temperature in the woodstove," she said. "Nothing to worry about. We do this all the time."

Mr. Pease came over to take a closer look at

the oven. "I didn't realize being a ship's cook was so complicated."

Ace removed the tray of smoking cookies and set them on the counter. "Man, look at these mothers. They've been cremated. And the ham! Looks like a meteor I saw once in the Smithsonian."

Stephanie squinted at the smoldering ham. "It is sort of black. Maybe it just needs basting," she said hopefully. She poked at it with a long-handled fork. "Probably we should pick the ashes off it first." She closed the oven door and checked the gauge. Five hundred degrees. She gave it a whack with the fork to make sure it was working. "Darn." She turned to Ace. "Any other ideas?"

Ace put his dark glasses back on. "It looks better this way."

The first mate looked in at them. "Stephanie here? Captain wants to see her."

Stephanie handed the fork over to Ace. "Does he make people walk the plank?"

Ivan unconsciously gripped the wheel a little tighter when he saw Stephanie. She had a sweat stain running down the center of her tank top, her hair was plastered against her damp forehead, her face was flushed under a layer of soot and flour, and cookie dough clung to her shirt and shorts. She caught sight of a pelican fishing the shoreline and stopped in her tracks. A wondrous smile lit her face, leaving no doubt in Ivan's mind that this was the first time she'd seen a pelican in flight.

She turned and waved at Ivan. "It's a pelican!" she shouted.

Ivan took a quick breath as emotion knifed through him. It was unnatural, he thought—the way she could knock the wind out of him with a simple wave and smile. Maybe unnatural wasn't precisely right, maybe supernatural was a better choice. What else would explain the instant attraction, the surge of joy at sharing a pelican sighting? Hell, he didn't even like pelicans. They were big, dumb, ugly, brown birds. He shook his head. He was losing it. Stephanie Lowe was making him crazy. She had him blaming a rise in his testosterone level on a defenseless three-hundred-year-old ghost.

"Did you see it?" she asked wide-eyed as she approached the helm. "I never realized they were so big."

He reached out with one hand and drew her beside him, feeling a rush of tenderness. "You

45

really are something," he said, plucking dried cookie batter from her hair. "I'm almost afraid to ask why you're head-to-foot soot. Could it have something to do with the black smoke that came billowing out of the galley five minutes ago?"

"A minor setback in my cookie making," Stephanie told him, trying to sound casual, almost swooning every time his fingertips touched her temple.

"How bad was the fire?"

"It was just some bags burning in the oven. I think we might even be able to eat the ham."

He did a fast mental assessment of their course, searching his mind for a night harbor that had a restaurant. "Was that Mrs. Pease I heard saying she was going to be burned to a crisp and drown?"

"She got a little excited." Stephanie put her hand on the wheel, feeling the polished wood slide under her fingertips.

"I guess I can relate to that," Ivan said, watching to see if she caught his implication. "Stephanie Lowe," he whispered, his voice a sexy growl, "you stir up the pirate blood in me."

"Omigod."

Ivan tipped his head back and laughed. It

had been the perfect response. It said it all. He motioned for Stephanie to take the wheel and stood behind her. "Now, my fair pirate's wench, time for thee to learn the ways of the ship."

"Are you kidding me? You mean I really get to drive?"

"No, you don't get to 'drive.' You get to *steer*. And while you steer, we can talk."

"If I'm the one steering, why are you still hanging on to the wheel?" .

Ivan pressed himself lightly into her back and murmured into her hair, brushing his lips against the shell of her ear. "Because it's a sneaky way of getting you where I want you."

Stephanie closed her eyes and swallowed as a combination of panic and desire rushed through her. He was good. She had to give him that. He'd made sure everything was right up front in a voice that sounded like rustling sheets. So what's next? She wanted new experiences. How about a roll in the hay with a scoundrel? She cringed at the word *scoundrel*. Six months ago she would have said *jerk*. Now here she was thinking about ghosts and pirates and scoundrels. And romance.

She supposed those were the things her

move to Maine was all about. She needed some fun and some whimsy in her life. She needed to make friends. And maybe she needed to have a real honest-to-goodness love affair. She was pretty sure a romance with Ivan Rasmussen wasn't a good idea—but nature seemed to be taking its course in spite of her misgivings.

Ivan tugged at Stephanie's hair. "Do you feel it, Steph?" he asked. "What do you suppose this is between us? Lust? Love? Magic?"

The huge sails rattled, and Ivan spun the wheel to change direction and catch the wind.

Stephanie licked her lips, tasting the salt spray that bathed her face when the boat bit into the sea. "It's too soon for love, I hardly know you!"

"What about love at first sight?"

"Love at first sight is lust."

"Okay," he said. "What about lust at first sight? Are you in lust?"

"Definitely not!"

He grinned down at her. "Liar."

He liked her bravado and her ability to go forward, and for the first time in two months he felt at ease with his decision to sell Haben. Somehow, he knew it had fallen into the right

hands. Whether Aunt Tess thought so was another issue.

Stephanie turned to face him. "We haven't
touched on magic."

"Magic is a definite possibility. Any ghost
who would stoop to screwing up a toilet
wouldn't hesitate to mess with people's lives."

He looked dangerous when he smiled like
that, Stephanie thought. He was teasing—on
many levels. It was darned unnerving, and the
beard served as the perfect foil for a smile that
would have been a definite tip-off to Little Red
Riding Hood. Worst of all, she couldn't tell
where the teasing ended, but she suspected he
actually did believe in ghosts.

Chapter 3

Stephanie sprawled on the polished fo'c'sle roof and stared at the black sky and bright stars. There aren't stars like this over Jersey City, she thought. Jersey City had too many lights of its own to be bothered with stars. And if you did see stars, they weren't close like Maine stars. Jersey City stars were remote, because nature was remote in Jersey City. Jersey City was loud and vital and had great pizza parlors, but you'd be hard-pressed to find a stand of virgin pine. Stephanie closed her eyes and admitted to herself that she definitely missed the pizza. You didn't just wipe away your old life and start over without a few misgivings, and there had been times in the past two months when she thought she might have made too drastic a change in her lifestyle. Probably she should have moved to Connecticut for a couple of years, bought a few things from L. L. Bean, *then* moved to Maine.

It was the house that had pushed her into it, she decided. When she was nine years old she'd spent the summer with Lucy in Camden and had carried the fascination with the big white house with her ever since. It was one of those bits of baggage that forever floated loose in the mind, surfacing during moments of boredom, triggering fits of fantasy and vague discontent.

Even though she hadn't known the history of the house, it had conjured up images of black-frocked, bearded sea captains and their patient wives. She'd recently learned that it had been built in 1805 on the foundation of Red Rasmussen's lair. It was a magnificent huge box of a house, with a handsome cupola surrounded by a picket-fenced widow's walk. It had high ceilings with elaborate plaster medallions, black marble fireplaces, elegant moldings, and woodwork that had been carried by schooner from the mahogany forests of South America.

It sat on a hill overlooking Camden Harbor and was frequently wreathed in fog. It was a house that had weathered hurricane winds,

sleet, and snow and had not succumbed to aluminum siding. To a nine-year-old from New Jersey, it had seemed very romantic and exciting. When Stephanie reconsidered it at twenty-nine, it was Haben's endurance that impressed her the most. Haben was a survivor. It had been built with quality and pride. It felt stable to her at a time when her life was looking shaky.

Ivan stood watching Stephanie. She has secrets, he thought. She could be disarmingly candid, and yet he had the feeling she was guarding something. She reminded him of a cat that was always listening. Behind the good humor was a constant wariness. It wasn't cynical, he decided, but rather a kind of mental and physical alertness, as if she continually waited for something to happen. He had a fleeting thought that he might be the cause of all that tension, but quickly discarded it. Don't flatter yourself, Rasmussen, he mused, this woman's been up against something a lot more dangerous than your pirate routine.

She was lying flat out on the deckhouse roof, but she wasn't relaxed. Ivan felt his heart constrict with the suspicion that she probably hadn't relaxed in so long she'd lost the ability to do so.

Ivan saw her eyelids flutter open and knew he'd been detected even though he hadn't made a move or uttered a sound. The woman had radar. The man who married her would never get away with anything. It was a disconcerting thought. He'd known her for approximately ten hours, and he was thinking about marriage. It was Aunt Tess, he decided. She was getting even with him for selling the house. "I'm a bachelor," he mumbled under his breath. "I like being a bachelor. Get off my back!"

Stephanie propped herself on one elbow and looked at Ivan. "Were you mumbling at me?"

"I was talking to Aunt Tess."

"She always sails with you?"

"Never."

Stephanie raised her eyebrows. "This is a special occasion, huh?"

"I'm beginning to think so."

She sat up and swung her legs onto the deck. "This conversation is making me nervous. Is it leading up to something?"

"Not if I can help it."

"Hmmm," she said, throwing him the cool, appraising look she'd cultivated for teenage con men and twelve-year-old drug dealers. "Okay, then we have an understanding."

"Yup." He eyed her with a critical squint. "Just exactly what are the terms of this understanding?"

Stephanie fidgeted. Darned if she knew. She just wanted to steer the conversation away from ghosts and sex. She didn't feel especially brave or knowledgeable about either of those subjects. "I thought the terms were obvious."

"No involvement?"

"Right," Stephanie said, "no involvement. Physical or otherwise." Then she smiled at him. It was too late. They were up to their armpits in involvement.

Ivan smiled back at her. "As the blood relative of Red Rasmussen, I feel it my cavalier obligation to lie once in a while to a pretty woman. What's your excuse?"

"My father's grandmother was a Hungarian Gypsy. My great-uncle Fred defected from the army. My great-grandfather's brother was hanged for rustling."

"That explains it."

Stephanie woke up with a start and fell off the edge of her narrow bunk onto the padded bench seat and ultimately onto the cold wood plank floor. She instinctively rolled into a crouch and reached for her gun. When she didn't find it tucked into the sweats she was using as pajamas, she stayed perfectly motionless while her mind scrambled to place her in the proper environment. The room was black as pitch and unfamiliar. She'd been having a nightmare, and now she was awake—almost.

"I've heard of people jumping out of bed before, but you've got them beat. I especially liked the way you reached into your pajamas. Dreaming about me?"

Stephanie groaned when everything clicked into place. She was on a boat. It was the middle of the night. And for some yet-to-be-explained reason, Ivan Rasmussen had awakened her. She pulled herself up and blinked at him. "Did you wake me?"

"Time to get up, Sleeping Beauty. Time to get the stove stoked up. Time to get the coffee going. Time to bake the pies."

"You have a death wish? Is your insurance paid up?"

Ivan lit an oil lamp, casting the cabin in a soft glow. "Can I choose my method of death?"

She put her nose to the ship's clock on the cabin wall. "It's five o'clock!"

"Yeah. I let you sleep an extra half hour."

Love Overboard

"Ace told me Lucy got up early to bakes pies but I thought he was kidding."

Ivan lit two more oil lamps. "Sometimes she bakes cheesecake."

"Listen, Ivan, I've seen those people up on deck. They're not in such good shape. They don't need the calories. They shouldn't have the cholesterol. There's nothing wrong with having an apple for dessert," she said, crawling back into her bunk.

Ivan grabbed her by the ankle but released it when she growled. She sounded as though she meant business! He considered his options. He could do the caveman thing and haul her out, or he could do the pirate thing and crawl in next to her, or he could do the cowardly thing and try to lure her out with a bribe.

Ten minutes later, Stephanie opened one eye and sniffed the air. Coffee. She pulled the covers over her head and burrowed under her pillow, but the aroma of coffee crept under the bed linens. "Crud." He was playing hardball. "Coffee," she croaked out. "I want coffee."

Ivan threw another log into the woodstove. "You have to get up to get it."

Stephanie dragged herself out of bed and lurched across the room. "Sneaky, aren't you?"

"Yup."

She brushed the hair out of her face and took a mug of steaming coffee from him. "Rasmussen men leave something to be desired, do you know that?"

Ivan poured himself a cup of coffee and grinned at her. "Most women find Rasmussen men to be irresistible."

"Irresistible is different from less than perfect." She looked over at Ace's empty bunk. "Where's my partner in crime? Did he jump ship?"

"He's been up since four-thirty, like a good galley helper, but he was afraid to wake you. He says you talk in your sleep about shooting people."

Stephanie lowered her eyes and sipped her coffee. "Guess I've been watching too much television."

Ivan stared at her, wondering if she actually shot people. He remembered the way she'd rolled under the table, crouched, and reached behind her out of instinct, and he felt a chill race down his spine. She said she was twenty-nine, but she looked more like nineteen, her youthful appearance only adding to his unease, making him feel ridiculously protective.

People shot other people in self-defense, but she didn't look battered or persecuted. Criminals shot people. He knew she wasn't a criminal. There was one other possibility. She mentioned earlier that she was sort of a teacher in a government program. Ivan thought that was a stretch. "You're a cop, aren't you?"

She felt her heart stop, then start beating again, very deliberately. Thud, thud, thud. Lord, when would the panic leave her? How many years would it take before that question didn't make her whole life flash before her eyes? She took a deep breath and kept her voice low and steady. "I *was* a cop."

She said it with a finality and tone that didn't encourage further discussion. Her mouth was drawn tight, and her gaze held his, challenging him to make a flip remark. He thought of her rolling down the hill and cooking fish-eye soup and got an immediate mental image of Stephanie Lowe starring in one of those goofy *Police Academy* movies. Then the image changed. He watched the play of emotions on her face and knew she'd been a better cop than cook. Probably one of the best. And he also knew something terrible had happened to her.

"You don't want to talk about it, do you?"

"No."

"Everyone has secrets on a pirate vessel," he said. "It's allowed."

Stephanie felt the tears hot behind her eyes and blinked them back in a rush of relief that Ivan hadn't asked any more questions.

"I really should go look for Ace," Ivan said. "He has a knack for worming his way into a warm bed. He's probably snuggled next to a sympathetic female body by now, handing her some pathetic line about being an orphan or being a virgin or being abducted by Martians when he was eight."

Stephanie smiled at the obvious affection and resigned humor in Ivan's voice. He was doing a good job of lightening the conversation, and she appreciated it. "Any of it true?"

"He's the pampered son of a corporate lawyer. He isn't an orphan. He isn't a virgin. And to the best of my knowledge he was never abducted by Martians."

"You like him, huh?"

"Yeah. He's an okay kid. He reminds me a lot of myself at his age." He looked at Stephanie and grinned. "I thought I was pretty hot stuff when I was nineteen. Anyway, his dad's a friend of mine, and he asked me to take Ace on for the summer as a favor."

"Ace has been in some trouble," Stephanie guessed.

"He's had problems. I think he's straightening out."

Stephanie gave Ivan a long, considering look. She liked him for keeping Ace's problems confidential, and she liked him for trying to help by giving Ace a job. She hadn't expected Ivan the Terrible to have any substance, and it left her momentarily stunned when she realized Ivan might understand what she'd done with her life. She knew she'd have to wrestle with that later.

She'd also have to think about prejudging men on the quality of their buns. She'd underestimated Ivan Rasmussen because his jeans curved in all the right places. She was afraid to ask about his education. He'd probably graduated *magna cum laude* from Harvard Law School.

She moved closer to the stove to warm her bare feet and refill her coffee cup, feeling the caffeine kick in. "I'm awake," she announced. "Now I'm going to make pies." She hitched up her sweats and gave Ivan a brazen smile. "I might even make one that's edible."

Someone screamed from the back of the ship, and Stephanie felt her skin crawl at the sound of raw terror. She bolted up the galley stairs and headed for the aft cabin, where she found Mr. Pease trying to calm his wife.

Loretta Pease saw Ivan enter the cabin behind Stephanie and directed her attention to him. "I was almost killed, right here in this bed. By a woman. Skippy had gotten up to visit the facilities, and this woman just glided in and looked right at me. Wasn't one of the passengers either. I know all the passengers. Scared me half to death. She was all in black, with her hair done up on top of her head, and she was holding a knife."

"Sometimes Loretta likes to take a nip of sherry to start the day off right," Mr. Pease told Ivan.

"I didn't have a nip of sherry, you old coot. I'm telling you, there was a woman here."

Stephanie took the older woman's hand and began collecting information. Loretta Pease was obviously shaken. Her face had been white when they'd arrived, but color was flooding back into it now. Her palm was moist, her hand unsteady. Her glasses were neatly lying on the shelf above the small sink,

Stephanie noticed. She remembered Mrs. Pease had pushed her glasses down her nose and looked over them to search for the fish eye in her soup. That meant she was nearsighted. Coupled with the fact that the cabin was dark, it meant she probably hadn't gotten a very good look at the woman. "Did this person touch you or say anything to you?" Stephanie asked.

"No. She just stood there with this *big* knife."

"Can you tell me approximately how old she was?"

"It was too dark. I couldn't see her face well, but I swear, she had the biggest knife I've ever seen. A great big carving knife. Do I smell coffee?"

"You bet," Ace said, popping into the cabin. "Fresh brewed aboard the *Josiah Savage*. Everyone can come below and get some, drink up, then we'll search the vessel to flush out this woman from hell."

"The coffee was a good idea, but I think we could soft-pedal the woman from hell stuff," Ivan told him.

"Just an expression," Ace said affably.

Stephanie held Mrs. Pease's plump hand. "Why don't you get dressed and come down to

63

the galley? You can have some coffee and help me make blueberry muffins for breakfast."

An hour later Ivan dropped in to see how the baking was going. He told himself he was checking on Loretta Pease, but he knew it was a lie. Stephanie Lowe fascinated him as no other woman ever had. She'd been a cop! So how did he feel about that, he asked himself. A little threatened? Definitely. And very curious, and very aroused, and oddly pleased. It seemed to suit her. He picked a clump of muffin dough out of Stephanie's hair. "You're a mess."

"Flatterer."

He poured a cup of coffee. "Everything okay here?"

"We've made enough muffins to feed the whole Pacific fleet," Mrs. Pease said, taking a big basket of warm muffins topside.

Ivan sipped his coffee. "Ace and I have searched the ship and haven't turned up anything unusual."

Stephanie followed his gaze to the butcher block knife holder and gave him a silent affirmation that his discovery was correct. There was a knife missing.

She moved next to him and kept her voice

low while she filled the last muffin tin. "It's suspicious but hardly conclusive. I'm not familiar enough with the galley to be sure the knife is missing. Lucy could have lost it or misplaced it."

He stared at her for a minute, absorbing the pleasure of being near her, feeling the need to tease her out of her self-imposed silence about her past. He didn't want to be shut out. He'd go very slowly, he decided. He'd keep it light until she felt comfortable. "Were you like Eddie Murphy?"

"What?"

"You know, *Beverly Hills Cop*. Did you go around sticking bananas in people's tailpipes?"

Stephanie smiled. "Figuratively, yes."

"And as a former professional, what do you make of this?"

"I think Mrs. Pease saw something. I'm not sure what."

Ivan nodded. "Whatever it was, it vanished into thin air."

Stephanie stood statue still, a spoonful of dough poised over the batter bowl. "Like a ghost? Aunt Tess have any homicidal tendencies?"

Ivan shook his finger at her. "Don't even think it! 'Vanished into thin air' is just a figure of speech. Aunt Tess doesn't go skulking around wielding carving knives. She's a nice old lady. Besides, ghosts don't look human. They're . . . gauzy or something."

"Have you ever seen one?"

"Well, no, not actually."

Stephanie put the last batch of muffins in the oven. "Then how do you know what they look like? For that matter, if you've never seen a ghost, how can you be sure your house is haunted?"

"My mother's seen Tess."

Stephanie raised her eyebrows.

"Tess only shows herself to women." Ivan took a warm muffin and broke a piece off. "That's the legend. Only the women of Haben have seen her. And not all of the women. She's picky about who she scares." He popped the piece of muffin into his mouth and chewed appreciatively. "These are good!"

"You sound surprised."

"Mrs. Pease must have made them."

"Boy, that really hurts." She put the bowl into the sink to be washed and pushed her hair behind her ears, wondering about the legend, wondering if she believed it. "We have muffins and coffee on deck at seven, right?" Stephanie asked Ivan. She unconsciously caught the tip of her tongue between her teeth and stared at him, only partially listening to his answer, her mind still occupied with thoughts of ghosts.

He grinned at the fresh swipe of batter clinging to her bangs. "Yup. And full breakfast in the galley at eight." He took a tray and began arranging mugs on it. "So, what do you really want to know?"

Stephanie wiped her hands on her sweatpants and realized with a start that she'd been telegraphing her inattention. There'd been a time when she would never have dared do that. Now, there was Ivan, seeing right through her, and she was loving it. It was a good feeling. All those years of evasive answers and role-playing and never letting down her guard were behind her, thank heaven. She'd lost patience with it. She wasn't all that good at relaxing yet, but she was getting better. "Do you honest-to-goodness believe this Aunt Tess business?"

Ivan fed her a piece of his blueberry muffin. "This is not the time or place to discuss such mystic matters. I think we need to arrange a rendezvous."

"A simple yes-or-no answer would be fine."

"A simple yes-or-no answer wouldn't be nearly enough. First of all, you should talk about spooky things when it's dark. Everybody knows that. And fog helps a lot." His gaze dropped to her mouth. "And a little moonlight wouldn't be a bad idea either."

"Moonlight talk always makes me nervous."

He fed her another piece of muffin and purposely stroked her lower lip with his fingertip. "It's my duty as the descendant of a famous pirate to make women nervous once in a while."

"Gee, Red would be proud of you."

He pinned her against the counter. "Red would think I was a wimp. You know what real pirates did to their women?" he whispered, letting his lips brush against the sensitive skin just in front of her earlobe.

Stephanie shivered in anticipation.

"They ravished them," Ivan told her. "It wasn't a pretty sight."

"That's it? No details?"

Ivan threw her a stern look. "You're not cooperating here. You're supposed to be intimidated."

"You know what intimidates me? The thought of making breakfast. According to Lucy, I'm supposed to whip up a cauldron of oatmeal, three dozen eggs, and seven pounds of bacon."

"Sounds about right." He took the tray of mugs and turned toward the stairs. "I'll meet you on the poop deck tonight at ten, Cinderella. Wear something appropriate for ravishing."

At ten o'clock Stephanie took the last of the blueberry pies out of the oven and damped down the fire. Now she knew why Lucy made pies first thing in the morning. If you tried to make them in the afternoon, when the ship was under way, the filling slopped over the sides and baked on the bottom of the stove. So you had your choice of making them at night or making them in the morning. Since Stephanie wasn't a morning person, she'd decided to make them at night.

She looked down at herself and took an inventory of everything she'd cooked: oatmeal, spaghetti sauce, cookie batter, blueberry pies, and coffee. Wonderful. And she hadn't washed her hair since the previous morning or changed out of the sweats she'd slept in the night before. On the positive side, she'd cooked a damned good dinner of fried chicken, biscuits, green beans, and corn on the cob. Cooking wasn't much different from police work, she concluded. It required concentration, imagination, hard work, a little technical knowhow . . . and luck. She looked longingly at her bunk, wanting nothing more than to crawl behind the red curtain and sleep for at least a year. Unfortunately, Ivan was waiting for her on deck.

Ivan levered himself down the galley stairs, a slow smile spreading across his face as he took in the sight of Stephanie Lowe at the end of her first full day aboard the *Savage*. "I got tired of waiting, so I thought I'd come check things out. Pretty tough job, huh?"

"A hot shower, and I'll be good as new."

"I have a better idea. What you need after a long day of slaving over a scorching stove is a moonlight swim. Cool, refreshing . . ." Erotic, he added to himself.

A moonlight swim sounded great. Too bad she didn't have the strength to drag herself up the galley steps. "It's a lovely idea, but I'd sink like a stone. I'm exhausted. I'm afraid I'm going to have to opt for the shower."

Ivan slung his arm around her shoulders. "Honey, this is a carefully restored nineteenth-century schooner. We don't have a shower."

"Oh Lord, no shower." She slumped against him. "I have blueberry batter in my hair and spaghetti sauce soaked right through to my underwear, and you're telling me we don't have a shower?"

If she'd been alone, she probably would have burst into tears. She would have cried for all the kids she wasn't able to save from drugs. She would have cried for the Steve she never knew. She would have cried for all the times in the past eight years when she had desperately needed to cry and wasn't allowed that luxury. But she wasn't alone, and she had too much pride to cry in front of a man she'd known for only two days. Besides, she wasn't a woman who cried over spaghetti sauce. Usually she found a well-aimed expletive to be much more satisfying than indulging in tears. "So you suggest swimming, huh?"

"Did you bring a bathing suit?"

Stephanie sighed. She didn't even *own* a bathing suit. Narcs in Jersey City didn't lounge around at poolside waiting for middle-class crime, and they couldn't afford fancy vacations.

Ivan grabbed the bottle of dish-washing detergent from the sink and pulled Stephanie to the stairs. "From the sound of that sigh, I take it the answer is no." He pushed her up the stairs and stood beside her on the deck. "Are you the modest type?"

"My gynecologist asks that same question once a year, then he makes me sit in a freezing cold room wearing nothing but a paper jacket."

"What a brute. This is going to be much more fun."

Stephanie looked over the side of the ship at the still, black water. "You're not expecting me to skinny-dip, are you?"

"How bad do you want to get clean?"

The deck was empty and dark except for the soft glow of light escaping up the cabin hatches. The air was cool and heavy with the smell of the sea. The water lapped gently against the sides of the ship. It was inviting and scary as hell. "Can you keep the crowds of thrill seekers away?"

"Absolutely."

"And what about you?" she asked. "Are you swimming?"

"No. I'm ogling. Besides, I'm in charge of crowd control, remember?"

"Crowd control, yes. Ogling, no. How do I do this? It looks like a long way down."

"The yawl is tied behind us. Just use the stern ladder. You can get undressed in the yawl and quietly slip into the water." He handed her the bottle of dish detergent. "Use this to wash your hair. It won't get gummy in seawater."

He watched her go over the gunwale and scale the side of the ship like a cat burglar. Lithe, silent, efficient. He admired her style and, at the same time, hated the knowledge that it was probably a talent she'd acquired in dark, garbage-strewn alleys in seedy neighborhoods. He'd like to believe she'd directed traffic in front of a grade school or had had a nice, boring desk job, but he instinctively knew differently, and he felt his gut knot at the thought of her going toe-to-toe with drug dealers and the slime they fed off.

Stephanie settled herself in the boat and removed her shoes. "Turn your back," she called to Ivan, thinking he looked like the Cheshire cat with his rascally smile floating in the shadows of the night. "I'm not getting undressed with you staring at me."

I'm not much of a pirate, he thought, back turned. A real pirate would be down there in the boat with her . . . or at least sneaking a peek when she wasn't looking. He heard her sweats drop to the floor of the yawl and the soft splash of her hitting the water. And then the scream. His heart slammed against the wall of his chest, and in an instant he was over the gunwale, flying down the rope ladder. He reached the boat just as her head bobbed to the surface. "Holy Toledo!" she said, gasping. "This is cold! You miserable excuse for a human being, why didn't you tell me it would be this cold? And what are you doing in the boat?"

Ivan put his hand to his heart. "You screamed! I thought . . . I thought Jaws got you."

Several passengers looked down at Stephanie and Ivan.

"What's going on?" Mr. Pease wanted to know. "Are we interrupting anything?"

"It was the knife killer, wasn't it?" Loretta Pease asked. "Soon as I heard that scream, I knew it was the knife killer striking again."

Ivan looked up at her. "No, it wasn't the knife killer. It was just Cookie taking a bath."

"At this time of the night?"

"She had blueberry batter in her hair," Ivan explained. "You can all go back to bed now."

"Great crowd control," Stephanie said. "Maybe we should have sold tickets."

Ivan grinned at her and poured a glob of

dish detergent on the top of her head. "Hold on to the edge of the boat, and I'll wash your hair."

She looked at him suspiciously. "Can you see below the water?"

"Do you expect the descendant of a pirate to answer that honestly?"

Chapter 4

Stephanie ducked her head back to rinse out the soap and pushed herself away from the yawl. The water was tolerable, now that she was used to it, and she stroked out, enjoying the sensual freedom of swimming naked.

"Don't swim too far," Ivan called. "The cold is going to sneak up on you."

She waved to acknowledge his warning and swam parallel to the ship for a few more minutes before returning to him with chattering teeth. "Is the p-p-person in charge of crowd control also in charge of towels and d-d-dry clothes?"

"I knew I forgot something." He looked at her hopefully. "You could always air-dry."

"You know what you are? You're a p-p-pervert. Turn around while I get into the boat. I'll put my sweats back on."

"Sacrilege." He faced the side of the ship. "It's a crime against nature to cover that beautiful, clean body in spaghetti-stained sweats— especially the mole."

Stephanie pulled the shirt over her head and struggled into the pants. "That mole is in a private place!"

"And it's very pretty," he said softly.

She didn't know whether she was pleased or furious. She really should be mad at him, but there was something about the tone of his voice that touched her. It wasn't lewd or suggestive or even calculating. She couldn't see his face, but she knew he was smiling. A small, gentle smile, as if his world had suddenly turned beautiful because she had a mole on her backside. "Thank y-y-you," she said.

"We have to get you warm. Can you make it up the ladder?"

"This is nothing," she said. "Last February I was thrown into the Hudson River."

He caught up with her on the deck and whirled her around by her shirtsleeve. "I want to know about it."

Even in the dark, Stephanie could see that his eyes were hard. His mouth was drawn tight, and a muscle worked in his jaw. She blinked at him in surprise, confused by his emotional reaction. "It was c-c-cold."

"Damn." He picked her up and carried her to the galley, where he set her down in front of the stove. He checked the bunks to make sure they were empty and pulled the hatch cover shut. "Get those wet things off." He grabbed a large towel, a pair of thick socks, and a set of clean sweats from the shelf above her bed and returned to her, obviously disgusted at finding her still fully clothed. He muttered something indiscernible and unceremoniously stripped her sodden shirt over her head.

"Hey!" Before she could get anything else out, Ivan had stuffed her into the clean sweatshirt. He had his hands on the waistband of her pants when she instinctively gave him a knee to the groin and knocked him backward with a follow-up kick to the chest. He rolled over in pain and took several quick gasps of air before he was able to regulate his breathing. Stephanie groaned out loud and rushed to his side. "I'm sorry! I didn't mean to do that! It was a reflex."

Ivan closed his eyes, trying to relax. The pain in his groin was subsiding to the point where it wasn't nearly as bad as the cramp in his ego.

He'd just been trashed by a 120-pound woman. When he'd heard she'd gotten dumped in the river, he'd almost gone blind with rage, all his protective instincts for her welling to the surface. And then this poor, defenseless creature had leveled him!

Stephanie dabbed at his damp forehead with the towel. "Are you okay? You aren't permanently damaged, are you?"

"Do you care?"

"Of course I care!"

"Swell." He realized he was pouting and burst out laughing. He wasn't a man with a frail self-image. Now that the pain was reduced to a dull ache, he found more humor than humiliation in the incident. "When I was a kid and I skinned my knee, my mother always kissed it to make it better."

Stephanie hit him over the head with the towel.

He slowly got to his feet and turned his back to her. "If I were you, I'd hurry up and change while I'm still recovering."

She did as she was told in record time. "I'm all dressed," she said, tugging at the socks.

He handed her a cup of hot coffee and waited patiently while she sipped. He took the cup from her and towel-dried her hair until it was just slightly damp and completely unruly. He was standing very close to her, feeling ridiculously tender. She instilled the strangest feelings in him, he thought, feelings that were way beyond what they should be. They were wrapped in a pleasant intimacy that he'd never before experienced with a woman. And that intimacy was fueling a passion that was frightening in its intensity. He was trying to cover it with a flirting, casual attitude, but he didn't know how much longer he could get away with it. His body was going to betray him if he wasn't very, very careful.

He added a few logs to the stove to keep the fire burning and was relieved to see the color flooding back into her cheeks. He shouldn't have allowed her to swim, but he'd been mesmerized by the sight of her gliding through the black water.

Stephanie felt as if she were glowing from head to toe. She'd never experienced anything like her moonlight swim, and she'd never had a man care enough about her to dry her hair. It wasn't just lust between them, she thought happily. He *liked* her. And she liked him. She reached for her mug of coffee and stared at the pies sitting on the countertop. She counted them twice. "There's a pie missing."

"Are you sure?"

"I could guarantee it. I gave these pies four of the best hours of my life. Man, this is the pits. A pienapper! How low can you go?"

"Maybe we should look on the positive side. At least they're not afraid to try your cooking."

She gave him a warning wrinkle of her nose. "You want to elaborate on that?"

Ivan grinned at her. "Not me. I try not to get drop-kicked more than once a day."

Stephanie grimaced. "I can't believe I did that."

"Now I know how you kept your virginity for so long."

"I was an undercover narcotics cop for eight years, and that's the first time I've ever had to use self-defense to keep my pants on." Ivan didn't say anything, but Stephanie suspected he was thinking of more practical methods of removing her clothes. Their gazes held for a long moment, until Stephanie sighed in defeat, acknowledging that she'd only prolonged the inevitable. Sooner or later, he was going to get her naked—or more than likely, she was going to get herself naked. She decided to change the subject and make him a peace offering. "Could I interest you in some pie?"

Ten minutes later they were sitting at the heavy oak table enjoying warm blueberry pie, when someone knocked on the closed hatch cover. "Anybody home?" a female voice called. "Do I smell fresh coffee and hot blueberry pie?"

A second female passenger made her way down the ladder. "Blueberry pie! Yum!"

Mr. and Mrs. Pease joined them along with several other people. Stephanie put another pot of coffee on to drip and brought out more plates.

"You know who would love this?" Mrs. Pease said. "Lena Neilson and her cabin mate, Elsie. Do you think I should go get them?"

"Yes," Stephanie said, "and you could see if Mr. Kramer and Mr. and Mrs. Dembrowski are awake." She cut two more pies into wedges, set them on the table, and returned to the stove.

Ivan stood beside her, slouched against the wood cabinet. "You like this, don't you?"

Stephanie laughed. "It's hard work being a ship's cook, but it's fun." She wiped her hands on her clean sweats, never thinking about the new blueberry stains she was acquiring. When she spoke she kept her voice low so the conversation didn't carry past Ivan. "I was a narc for a long time, and my world was really very small. My work environment was frantic. The station house was noisy and chaotic, with a bunch of dedicated, underpaid, overworked cops living on candy bars and coffee. When I wasn't at the station house, I was in a school that was even noisier and more chaotic. After a while you get to thinking all of it is normal. You wonder if the whole world lives on fast food and works eighteen-hour days."

"What about your family and friends outside of work? What about those Sunday chicken dinners?"

Stephanie cut another pie while she talked. "I had personal reasons for becoming a cop, but once I started working, the personal reasons weren't important anymore. It was the kids who were important. I liked them. They needed help. They needed someone to get the pushers far away from them. They needed education. They needed enough confidence in themselves not to succumb to peer pressure. It wasn't as if I was God and could solve all those problems, but I made a small contribution. Anyway, it was very consuming. I visited my family, but I *lived* in the high school hallways.

Then I woke up one day, looked in the mirror, and realized I was getting too old to pass for a teenager."

There was a lot more to it than that, but she didn't feel like relating it. They'd moved her from one school to another, prolonging her career. In the end, she'd almost been killed because she hadn't been smart enough to quit while she was ahead.

She shrugged away the memory of it. *Almost* killed didn't count, she told herself. Everything had worked out okay, and here she was, cutting pie.

"I've missed a whole chunk of my life," she said. "I spent my twenties masquerading as a teenager. I didn't mind that so much, but I did mind the rat race existence I'd become used to. When I quit the police force and did some long-overdue introspection, I found myself feeling absolutely starved for things that were wholesome. Clean air, healthy food, good people. The one thing I've missed at Haben has been the people. I haven't been able to open for business because of the repairs, and I've been lonely."

She handed him the pie to take to the table. "This is great. This is like a pajama party!"

Loretta Pease and Lena Neilson squeezed

down the galley stairs. "We saw her!" Lena shouted. "She was on the deck. She had the knife, and there was blood on it!"

Ivan started toward the stairs, but Lena stopped him. "Don't bother rushing up there," she said. "She's gone."

He moved aside for the rest of the passengers filing in for blueberry pie. "Where'd she go?"

"Disappeared. Poof," Lena said.

Mrs. Pease agreed. "It's true. We came up from Lena's cabin, and there she was, all dressed in black, just like last time. She was standing at the back of the ship with the knife, and when she saw us, she jumped overboard, but we didn't hear a splash." Loretta Pease gave an involuntary shudder. "I got a pretty good look at her this time. She was creepy-looking. Her skin was white as a sheet, and she had lots of hair that was wild and had a blue tint to it. She looked like pictures you see of people who've risen from the dead."

"And when we went to look over the rail, we couldn't find her," Lena said.

Stephanie checked the people in the room. Everyone was accounted for, including Ace and the first mate. They'd both come in with

Mr. Kramer. No one looked as if they'd been stabbed with a carving knife. "Maybe we should have a look around anyway," she said to Ivan.

"Okay, who gets pie? Who gets coffee?" Ace asked, taking over.

Stephanie and Ivan slipped away and walked the deck in silence while Ivan played the searchlight over every nook and cranny, along the gunwales, up the tall masts.

"You think Lena and Loretta were into the sherry?" he finally asked. "That part about the wild blue hair doesn't play."

"It's a little bizarre, but Loretta Pease doesn't strike me as a person who would make up stories."

Ivan skipped the light across the oak water casks and mahogany planking. "I don't like having some ghoul running around on my ship. And I like the part about the bloody carving knife even less."

"I don't like it either. I think, until we know otherwise, we have to assume she's dangerous, although my own personal instincts lean more in the direction of it being a prank. Of course, it could always be Aunt Tess. Or maybe it's a new ghoul? Ghosts in your bedroom, ghouls on your ship. You must be popular when Halloween rolls around."

"You think it could actually be a ghoul?"

Stephanie looked at him sideways. "Are you serious?"

"Does the thought of having a ghoul on board frighten you? Does it make you want to throw yourself into my strong arms for protection?"

"The thought of *you* believing in a ghoul frightens me. It makes me want to call the Coast Guard."

Ivan curled his hand around her neck, stroking the nape with his thumb. "I bet you go to horror movies and never scream. You're one of those people who sit there and say it's all done with special effects."

He had great hands, Stephanie thought. Warm and strong and clever. "It *is* all done with special effects."

He pulled her closer. "Hmmm. Do you believe in Santa Claus? The Easter bunny? The tooth fairy? Jaws?"

"Maybe Santa Claus . . ."

He leaned forward and kissed her. He'd intended the kiss to be light and provoking, but it immediately turned serious, devouring whatever good intentions he'd had up to that point. He set the flashlight aside and pulled her to him, needing to feel the length of her against his body.

Stephanie had wanted to be kissed. Ivan Rasmussen made her feel sexy in a wonderful way, and she wanted to explore that feeling. She liked the way his mouth moved over hers, coaxing, demanding, exciting. He wasn't stingy with his emotions, and he wasn't afraid to put himself on the line. She liked that, too. Their tongues touched, and her hands roamed his smooth, muscled back.

She was losing it. Losing control, losing perspective. It happened when you fell in lust, and she knew she was in lust. No big deal, she told herself. People fell in lust all the time, and it was all right as long as you didn't mistake it for something more serious.

She leaned backward to look at him. "So this is what I've been missing all these years."

"This is nothing. It gets better as you go along."

She didn't doubt him for a second. "How far along do you think we should go?"

He studied her for a moment. "I'll let you decide that."

"My original plan was to save myself for marriage."

"Is this a proposal?"

Stephanie laughed. "No. Marriage seems a little drastic. I'm thinking of changing my game plan."

Her hand strayed to the rope rigging at her side, and her fingers closed around a coil that felt oddly sticky. She brought the hand forward and stared at it. Curiosity was replaced by horror, crawling along her spine and knifing through her stomach. It was blood, she thought. Dark and fresh, staining her palm, seeping between her fingers. "Oh Lord," she whispered, her voice hoarse with revulsion. "It's blood."

Ivan took a closer look and smiled. "No. It's blueberry." He put a finger into his mouth and sucked on it. "Yum."

Stephanie put her hand to her head and closed her eyes until her heartbeat returned to normal.

Ivan stood beside her. "Are you okay?"

"We've got to stop kissing like that. It stops the oxygen flow to my brain. I thought it was blood."

"An easy mistake to make in the dark. Somebody's been by here with your pie."

Stephanie looked at him. "How did it get on the rigging?"

Ivan retrieved his flashlight. "I'd say the pie thief was also a slob. Hold on, Watson! I think I've got something." He reached behind the rope and found the carving knife. "The murder weapon," he said. "I can guarantee that this knife was used to murder your pie. As anyone can see, it's covered with blueberry blood."

"Gee, I don't know if I'm relieved or disappointed. I was sort of hoping it would turn out to be Aunt Tess."

"The blue-haired woman from hell must have ditched the knife when she jumped overboard." He flashed the spotlight over the side, sweeping it over the water and the yawl. "Now, that's an interesting piece of maritime equipment," he said, shining the beam on Stephanie's panties, draped across the yawl seat.

Stephanie felt a blush creep up her neck. "I was in a hurry." She swung a leg over the gunwale and quickly scrambled down to the boat. She'd retrieved the scrap of pink lace and had started up the ladder, when her eye caught a flash of movement through a cabin window. She carefully edged closer to get a better look and found herself staring into two large, black-rimmed eyes in a face framed by blue-and-green spiked hair.

Ivan leaned over the side. "What's going on?"

"I've found the woman from hell, and she's not dead—she's just punk. The ladies didn't hear a splash, because when Ms. Blue Hair jumped, she grabbed hold of the ladder and swung herself through the open cabin window. Was this cabin supposed to be empty?"

Ivan nodded. "We had a last-minute cancellation."

Stephanie pulled herself up to the deck and looked for a place to stash her panties. "I don't have any pockets," she said, examining her sweats.

Ivan took the panties from her and stuffed them into the front pocket of his jeans. "First we'll go belowdecks to meet our stowaway, then I think we'll have a talk with Ace."

"Jeez," the young woman said when they opened her cabin door, "you scared the bejeebers out of me. What were you *doing* out there? Don't you know it's rude to peep in people's private windows?"

"Ship's security," Stephanie said. "You're

under arrest. You stole my pie. Do you know how long it took me to make that pie?"

"I needed it. You get scurvy when you're on a ship if you don't eat pie."

"What were you doing in Mrs. Pease's cabin this morning?" Ivan asked her. "And how do you get your hair to look like that?"

"I went up to the ice chest to get some mayo for my sandwich, and when I came back, I accidentally walked into the wrong cabin. Man, can that old lady scream, or what?" She touched her hand to her hair. "You like my hair? I did it with spray paint and starch."

The stairs creaked, and Ivan turned in time to see a sneakered foot hastily withdrawn. "Ace!"

"Whoops," Ace said with a guilty smile. "I didn't want to disturb you."

Ivan motioned him forward. "Your friend, I assume?"

The girl moved next to Ace. "We're engaged. Hey, you're a ship's captain! You could marry us! Wouldn't that be great, Ace? We could get married right now."

Ace took his glasses off and looked at Ivan. "You couldn't do that, could you?"

Ivan grabbed him by the shirt, marched him

down the hallway, then yanked him into the captain's quarters and closed the door. "You brought that girl on board and promised her you were going to marry her?"

"Not in the beginning. In the beginning I just promised her a sandwich. But then things got . . . involved, and I needed a better promise. Hell, I couldn't help it. I'm a hotbed of teenage hormones."

"How old is she? Do her parents know she's with you?"

"She's *old*. Twenty-three. She plays second guitar in a rock band, but their bus broke down in Rockland, and they had to cancel their tour."

"You do this again, and I'm going to cancel *your* tour. I'm going to give you thirty seconds to apologize to that woman, then you're confined to quarters for the rest of the night. And at the crack of dawn I want her set ashore. And I expect you to provide her with cab fare back to Rockland."

Ace adjusted his glasses. "Do you think I could have a partial advance on my wages?"

Ivan reached into his pocket and, without thinking, pulled out the panties.

"I didn't see that," Ace said, accepting a twenty-dollar bill while Ivan stared at the dainty piece of lingerie dangling from his finger. "I swear, I didn't see a thing," he repeated. "And I won't tell anybody about what I didn't see. You can count on me," he said, slipping out the door and gently closing it behind him.

Chapter 5

Stephanie braced herself against the counter and took a firm hold on her bread dough. According to Lucy, Wednesday was turkey dinner with all the trimmings. But Lucy didn't know about the storm that was off the coast of Atlantic City and moving north. Lucy didn't know the stowaway, Melody, would refuse to set foot in the yawl and would insist on helping out in the galley. Lucy didn't know any of those things because Lucy had run off to get married. Stephanie shoved her fist into the dough. This was going to cost Lucy. This was not just a toilet. This was a whole new kitchen.

"Jeez," Melody said, "that's a lot of dough. And you put your hands in it. Gnarly."

"It's for crescent rolls. All we have to do is follow Lucy's recipe."

Melody studied the directions. "Looks like origami."

"You know how to do origami?"

"No."

Stephanie blew a wisp of hair from her forehead and grabbed the rolling pin. "I'll do the first batch, and then once we get it figured out, you can take over."

"Cool."

The ship plowed through heavy seas, and Stephanie took time to wedge the coffeepots behind an iron bar to keep them from jiggling across the stove.

Mrs. Pease looked up from her solitaire game. "What was that creaking? The boat isn't falling apart, is it? Do you think we're going too fast? Is there a speed limit out here?"

Mr. Pease sipped his coffee and grinned. "Now this is what I call sailing."

"Okay," Stephanie said, returning to the dough, "it looks like we roll a lump of this flat, and then cut it into strips, then triangles." She took one of the freshly cut triangles and made an attempt at shaping it into a rolled crescent. She looked at Melody. "What do you think?"

"It doesn't look like the picture."

Stephanie stared at it. "It sort of does. You

have to use your imagination." She wiped her hands on her jeans. "It's all yours."

Ivan ambled down the stairs and took a clean mug from a hook on the ceiling. "What a terrific day," he said. "Fantastic wind."

Stephanie glared at him. Easy for him to say, she thought. He was up there with his nose in the salt spray pretending to be a Viking. She was down here getting seasick, trying to keep Melody from slipping banned substances into the turkey dressing.

Ivan poured himself a cup of coffee and looked over Stephanie's shoulder. "Haven't seen you all day. You're not avoiding me, are you?"

"I've been cooking!" The ship lurched, lanterns swung on their hinges, and coffee splattered and hissed on the hot stove. "I don't know how much you're paying Lucy, but it's not enough." She bit her lip against the wave of nausea and decided she'd smelled enough brewing coffee to last a lifetime.

"You look a little pale," Ivan said. "Maybe you should get some air."

Mr. Pease smiled at them. "I think it's real nice that you two are getting married. Love on the high seas. That's romantic."

Ivan's left eyebrow cocked a fraction of an inch. "Getting married?"

Mr. Pease blinked. "Aren't you getting married? I heard you were getting married."

Mrs. Pease rolled her eyes at her husband. "You always jump to conclusions. You didn't hear they were getting married. You heard they were—" She stopped and flushed. "You heard they were very close friends."

Mr. Pease winked at Ivan. "Must be something to have pirate blood in you, huh?"

Ivan forced a tight grin. "Mmmm."

Melody looked up from her rolls. "So are you two sleeping together, or what?"

"We're just 'or what,'" Stephanie told her. She took a deep breath. "I really do need air."

Ivan followed her up and put a steadying arm around her while she hung on the ropes. When the color had returned to her face, and he could see she was taking some interest in the whitecaps skidding past them, he kissed the back of her neck.

"That's how rumors are started," Stephanie said.

"No one saw. I was very careful. And besides, rumors are started by Ace. I accidentally pulled your panties out of my pocket while I was giving him a lecture on morals last night."

Her first reaction was surprise. She'd forgotten about the panties. And then her sense of the ridiculous took over. She tipped her head back and whooped with laughter.

Ivan pretended to look serious. "This is no laughing matter. My honor has been compromised."

"Nonsense. Pirates are supposed to carry panties in their pockets."

"How about *your* honor?"

Good question. She thought about it for a moment and decided her panties had a legitimate reason for being in his pocket, so her honor was untarnished. The only possible repercussion might be that her image was prematurely improved. And a new image was pretty much inevitable. She'd been contemplating a shift in outlook. Her attitudes about permissive sex hadn't changed, but her qualifications for a partner had become more flexible. She had very special feelings for Ivan and wanted to explore those feelings further. She wasn't ready to make a decision yet, but she felt certain she'd know when the time was right to sleep with a man, and it wouldn't necessarily be the result of a marriage certificate.

She leaned back against the ropes and flashed him a brazen smile. "I'll just look at this as a trial run to see if I like being a fallen woman."

Ivan rested his head against hers and talked into her hair in the soft, rumbling voice that Stephanie had come to love. "Let me know what you decide."

Stephanie felt her mind go slack for a moment, then pull back. He wasn't just carelessly flirting anymore. He was making a serious overture at moving the boundaries of their relationship. And it was scary. She turned from him to give herself some space and studied the horizon.

Ivan pointed to a stretch of land dead ahead in the distance. "That's Holbrook Island. Castine is almost due north on the mainland. I'm taking a more inland route for the rest of the trip so we can see the autumn foliage and have some protection from the storm."

"Do you think the storm will be bad?"

"No. It's veering out to sea, but it will make the water choppy for a few days." He leaned back against the roof. "My great-great-grandfather sailed these waters in a schooner very much like the *Savage*. He transported lumber down the Penobscot River and throughout the bay. He's one of my favorite ancestors. He was a little boring compared to some others, but I think he must have led a quality life. I know from his diary that he took the time to see the sun set, and he enjoyed his family, and he built Haben."

Stephanie sat beside him, drawing her knees close to her chest, wrapping her arms around them. "Would you rather be hauling lumber than human cargo?"

He grinned. "Hauling lumber sounds like a job, and I'm a bum at heart. This is like being on a continuous vacation."

"What do you do in the winter?"

"Make repairs and improvements. Last winter I built the yawl." And last spring I worked twelve hours a day in a shoe factory, he thought. Not a memory he cherished. He wasn't a man who felt comfortable in large brick buildings. He hated ties, shaving, telephones, and pretty secretaries who called him Mr. Rasmussen.

A loud crash came from the galley. Stephanie and Ivan exchanged grimaces. A headful of blue-and-green hair popped out of the galley hatch, and Melody waved at Stephanie. "Don't worry. Everything's fine," Melody called. "I think we can still eat the turkey."

Stephanie waved back. "Keep up the good work."

Ivan smiled at Stephanie. "Melody makes you look like Betty Crocker."

"I feel as if I'm back doing police work."

"Does it bother you to have Melody on board? I can make more of an effort to get rid of her—"

"No. She really wants to finish the cruise. She lied to Ace about her age. She's only eighteen. Graduated from high school in June. But she was telling the truth about the band. She's from Scranton, and I don't think she saw too many options open to her. Her dad works in the mines, and her mother works as a grocery clerk. Several conservatories offered her a partial scholarship, but being on the road with a rock band sounded a lot more glamorous. From the way she's clinging to this ship, I'd guess she was relieved when the bus broke."

"You mean under all that blue-and-green hair we've got Julie Andrews?"

"Not exactly. Maybe Cher with a touch of Bette Midler and Shirley Temple."

"So you think we should keep her, huh?"

Stephanie sighed. "I'm a real sucker, I know. She's driving me nuts in the kitchen, but there's this little-kid vulnerability to her. I've seen so many teenagers just like her. They get hurt and feel helpless, and they rebel. They go out looking for easy answers to hard problems."

Ivan watched her, hoping she'd go on. He knew she was thinking about herself and her life as a cop. As a kid she'd probably taken in stray cats and rescued baby birds that had fallen from their nests. She was one of those people who stopped to remove turtles from the middle of the road and gave money to street people. And now she had another foundling, and it had to remind her of the life she'd tried to escape. "You're not thinking of adopting her, are you?"

Stephanie laughed. "She's too old to adopt, but I think I could share my fresh air with her for a while. Three months ago I couldn't have managed it. It's a little like looking in the rearview mirror and seeing where I've been—and deciding it wasn't such an awful

105

place. Not necessarily a place I'd want to return to, but a place I'm glad to have seen. And I'm a little shocked at how remote that previous life has become. I still have some bad dreams, and I haven't entirely lost the wary attitude I developed after years of undercover work, but I've discovered the top layer of disgust and burnout has all peeled away."

And a lot of it had happened since she came aboard the *Savage*, she thought. She was working hard, she was exhausted, and she was challenged. She liked the sea, the *Savage*, and everyone around her. She'd come to realize a lot about herself in the past two days. She wasn't a loner type. She liked noise and people and hugs and kisses. She felt terrifically alive and self-indulgent.

There was another crash, and Stephanie winced. "I'd better get back to the galley."

He held her wrist. "I'd like to continue our conversation later."

Stephanie wondered which part of the conversation he wanted to continue and felt a twinge of panic.

"Uh-oh, you look like you need to be talked into this," Ivan said, grinning. "Tell you what, if you come to my cabin at ten tonight, I'll show you my gyroscope."

"Gee, how could anyone refuse an offer like that?"

The sun was low, hidden behind a thick cloud cover when everyone sat down to the turkey dinner. The ship's anchor had been dropped in a protected cove, and the *Savage* lay motionless as a fine rain pelted against the windows and roofs. The gray dreariness of the sea and sky made the interior of the ship seem rich with creature comforts and alive with the energy of its inhabitants. Every lantern had been lit in the forward cabin. The air was heavy with the smell of roast turkey and sage dressing, and conversation and laughter filled the room, rising and falling like the comforting slap of waves against the wooden hull. Stephanie took her place at the table and almost went faint at the sight of the feast she'd created. It was wonderful. All modesty aside, she didn't think Lucy could have done a better job.

Mr. Pease helped himself to mashed potatoes and poured hot gravy over his turkey slices. "This is great. This is just like Thanksgiving."

Mrs. Pease studied her roll. "These rolls are delicious, and they're in so many different shapes. What a wonderful idea. This roll looks just like a . . ." Her face turned scarlet, and she dropped the roll onto her plate with a small gasp.

Mr. Pease looked at the roll. "It looks like a man's parts!" His face creased into a broad grin. "Daggone if it doesn't!"

Stephanie examined her own roll, then clapped a hand over her mouth to keep from laughing.

"I couldn't make crescents," Melody explained. "They kept falling apart."

Ace had removed his dark glasses. He had two rolls on his plate, side by side. "My rolls are in love," he said.

Melody glared at him with her raccoon eyes. "Your rolls aren't in love. Your rolls are in heat!" She waved her butter knife at him. "Your rolls should be emasculated, you little runt."

Ace put his glasses back on. "Hey, I don't go around making dirty rolls, do I? Noooooo. Is this the pot calling the kettle black?"

"You told me you loved me and wanted to marry me."

Ace sliced a piece of turkey. "Yes, but I didn't say when."

*   *   *

At ten o'clock Stephanie squared her shoulders and knocked at the door to Ivan's cabin.

"Couldn't resist getting a look at my gyroscope, huh?" he said, pulling her inside. His bed was perfectly made with a red plaid blanket and white sheets. The small electric cabin light was lit. He sat on the bed and patted the spot next to him.

Stephanie sat on the edge and folded her hands in her lap. "This isn't going to work. I feel uncomfortable. Probably everyone's standing outside your door listening."

"Probably everyone's sound asleep after that turkey dinner."

She shifted on the bunk and cracked her knuckles. "So, what do you want to talk about? Sex?"

"Gonna jump right in, huh?"

"Yeah." She took a shallow breath. "Let's get it over with."

"You sure you want to talk about sex?"

"Absolutely." She sprang to her feet and paced in the narrow cabin. "Sex has been on my mind a lot lately. I've been thinking about it all afternoon. So I figure I should get it out in the open. You know, get it off my chest."

"Uh-huh."

"Actually, I was wondering if . . . if you wanted to go to bed with me."

The subtle approach, Ivan thought, smiling. Was it any wonder he was crazy over her? "Is this a rhetorical question or a proposition?"

"I suppose it's a rhetorical question. Does that make a difference in your answer?"

She was contemplating having a romance, and he happened to be convenient, Ivan thought. Still, Stephanie wasn't the sort of woman to participate in indiscriminate sex. If she was considering a romance, that meant she'd decided she liked him. And that was good because he thought this relationship had real potential. Maybe it was the low-pressure weather that was affecting his mood. Or maybe it was the right time in his life. Or maybe Stephanie Lowe was simply the right woman. Whatever the reason, the bottom line was that he was a goner, Ivan admitted. He was in lust, but even worse, he suspected he loved Stephanie Lowe. Being in lust was the rush of passion that made your stomach flip and your gut knot up. It was novelty, excitement, a chase. Love was a more gentle emotion. And he was experiencing both.

He hadn't always been so discriminating in the past, but Stephanie had something special to offer him, and he wanted to make sure her first time was perfect. He didn't want her having any reservations or regrets. "Steph, any man would be a fool not to want to go to bed with you, but—"

"Here comes the *but*. That's what Steve said . . . *but*. You're not going to dump on me, are you?"

"No!"

"But you don't want to go to bed with me. I can tell you don't want to go to bed with me."

"Of course I want to go to bed with you, it's just that—"

"Yes?"

This was something that needed to be handled delicately. He searched for the right words and drew a blank.

"You aren't going to give me a lecture on loose morals, are you? Listen, Buster, I deserve to have a romance. I've hung on to my virginity for twenty-nine long years."

This wasn't going well. He sat up straighter and dragged a hand through his hair. "Stephanie, you don't want to rush into something like a romance just because you think

111

your bedpost needs some notches." Way to go, Rasmussen, really delicate. He grimaced. He couldn't believe he'd said that.

"Good grief."

"Sorry, but I'm new at this. I've never tried to talk a woman out of going to bed with me before."

"Lucky me. What an honor. In case you haven't noticed, I haven't completely decided to go to bed with you. Maybe I'll decide against it. Maybe I'll decide Ace is a better prospect. Maybe I'll decide to run an ad in the paper. Lord, I never thought it would be so hard to get rid of my virginity. Maybe I should rent a pervert."

"That isn't funny."

Stephanie plopped back onto the bed. "I might cry."

Ivan stuffed a pillow behind his back and pulled Stephanie against him, wrapping her in his arms. "Steph, do you trust me?"

She thought about it for a moment. "Yes."

"Don't worry about the sex."

"Easy for you to say." Stephanie sighed. "I've been afraid for so long, you know? I wanted to be brave about this. I wanted to . . . go for the gusto."

"What were you afraid of?"

"Everything. Just call me No Guts Stephanie. I lost my courage as a cop, then I realized that I didn't have any courage as a person. All those chicken dinners and meaningless evenings with Steve. I was like a little kid carrying around a security blanket. I was afraid to go off on my own, afraid to break away from my parents, afraid to take risks in a more demanding male-female relationship."

"Sometimes when you're very close to things, it's hard to see them. They get out of perspective. You were doing something that obviously was important to you, and you had to delay other parts of your life for a while. There's nothing wrong with that."

Stephanie allowed herself the luxury of leaning on him. "Thanks. I know it was a trade-off, but I think toward the end I was using my job as an excuse to avoid developing other areas of my life. I'd forgotten how to make friends. I'd made my life very narrow. I'd lost the courage to be accessible . . . to be vulnerable."

"And now?"

"There are so many things I want to do. I feel as though I've been standing with my nose pressed against the bakery window, and now

I'm finally allowed inside, and I don't know what to buy first."

"What goodies are at the top of your list?"

Stephanie hesitated. She shifted around in his arms and looked him straight in the eye. "I guess *your* goodies would be number one."

"Oh."

"*Oh?* That's all you can say? *Oh?* I've just told you for the second time in ten minutes that I'm hot for your goodies, and all you can say is *oh.* I've just spilled my guts about being vulnerable, and all you can say is *oh.* What kind of a pirate are you anyway? Why aren't you ravishing me? Why doesn't anyone ever want to ravish me?" She was shouting, and her cheeks were bright red. "Look at me! I'm hysterical! You've made me hysterical. I've never been hysterical before."

She took a deep, calming breath and pressed her lips together. "I'm going to leave now. Tomorrow I'm going to be mortally embarrassed about this, so I'd appreciate it if you wouldn't talk to me. In a year or so my embarrassment will probably fade, and maybe we can be friends. In the meantime, stay far away from me."

*   *   *

Stephanie sat Indian style on the forward cabin roof. She huddled inside her hooded sweatshirt and squinted into the drizzle. Everything around her was black. There were no stars, no moon, no light from belowdecks. Everyone was asleep, exhausted from an old-fashioned Maine clambake. Tomorrow they'd sail into Camden Harbor and go about their business. Tomorrow she'd hunt up Stanley Shelton and get her toilet fixed. And Sunday she'd sleep until noon. She saw a shadow move at the other end of the ship and realized Ivan was also on deck and watching her. She had mixed feelings about that. He hadn't done anything but watch her for three days. It wasn't any secret he was lying low. Of course, that was exactly what she'd ordered him to do, but it didn't sit well all the same.

He walked toward her, looking like an apparition gliding through the mist, very mysterious and a little spooky. He stood in front of her with his thumbs stuck in his jeans pockets. "Can't sleep?"

"Didn't want to."

"Making the most of your last night on board?"

"Something like that." The truth was, she

was restless. She'd wanted to have a ship-board romance and had only succeeded in making a spectacle of herself. So she'd come topside to sit in the rain and lick her wounds and feel sorry for herself. In the process she was thinking a few nasty thoughts about Ivan Rasmussen.

"I had a call from Lucy this evening. She said she'll be sailing with me on Monday."

Stephanie looked at him. There was laughter behind his gray eyes—and something else. He was holding something back. "And?"

"And she didn't get married."

"*What?*" Stephanie jumped to her feet. "What do you mean, she didn't get married? She's still engaged? What happened?"

"I guess they had a big fight, and Lucy told him what he could do with his plumbing."

"Oh, man. How could she do this to me? Is he going to fix my toilet?"

Ivan's mouth curved. "I don't know. Didn't sound to me as though they parted friends."

"I did this for nothing! I suffered through this whole dumb week for nothing!"

The smile faded from Ivan's lips, he grabbed her by the arms, and he pulled her to him. "I wouldn't say you did it for nothing."

Oh, great. Now he was going to deliver some little speech about ships passing in the night, she thought bitterly. He was going to give her one of those kisses that left her babbling nonsense, then he was going to say it was swell. Maybe she should introduce him to Steve. "Hmmm," she said. It was all she could manage, and even to her ears it sounded grim.

"Are you mad about something?" Of course she's mad, he thought. In her eyes, he'd rejected her, insulted her, and embarrassed her. And for the past three days he'd kept his distance, waiting for her to calm down, but it seemed as if she'd grown more furious with each passing day.

"No. Jeez, what would I be mad about? I propositioned you and was immediately rejected. But, hey, who's holding a grudge? All that talk about pirates ravishing pretty girls, then nothing. *Nothing!*" She spun away from him and stomped over to the rail. "I can't imagine why you think I'm mad."

"Maybe it's the way you're shouting and waving your arms."

"I'm *not shouting*."

Stephanie felt the shove of hands at her back and then she was flying through space and plunging feetfirst into the ocean. She bobbed to the surface sputtering expletives.

Ivan dropped a life preserver beside her. "Are you okay?"

"Do I look okay? I'm in the water. I'm drowning."

He dropped a rope ladder over the side and plunged into the water beside her. "Grab hold of the ladder and pull yourself up before you get dragged under by the weight of your clothes."

"Get away from me, you maniac. You tried to kill me."

"Listen, lady, I'm in freezing cold water, fully clothed, and I'm trying to rescue you. Now get up the stupid ladder."

Stephanie labored up the ladder and staggered onto the deck. "You pushed me! I should have you arrested for attempted manslaughter."

"I didn't push you. What's this thing you have about being pushed anyway? Someone pushed you down the hill and someone pushed you into the water. You know what I think? I think you're a fruitcake."

"You take one step closer, and I'm going to scream," she said to Ivan.

Ivan kicked off his shoes and wrung out his woolen shirt. "Now you're resorting to screaming? Don't you want to kick me in the groin? Maybe break a few bones?"

"Now that you mention it, maybe I do."

"Okay, come on."

Stephanie rolled her eyes.

Ivan grinned at her. "I'm waiting."

"This is ridiculous."

He stalked her around the forward deckhouse. He curled his finger at her. "Come here, Stephanie."

"Forget it. I'm not going to wrestle with you." More games, she thought. They'd roll around together until she was all bothered, then he'd probably pitch her back into the ocean to cool off. No thanks.

She turned on her heel and squished down the ladder to the galley. A single lantern cast a soft circle of light over the cabin. The fire in the stove was almost out. Stephanie stoked it to life and added several logs.

Ivan followed her down the stairs, looking over at Ace's bunk. "Doesn't he ever sleep in his own bed?"

"I think he's made up with Melody."

"They deserve each other."

Stephanie stepped out of her shoes and pulled the wet sweatshirt over her head, leaving her in a soaked T-shirt. And what about me? she wondered. Did she deserve Ivan Rasmussen? Wasn't Steve enough? She twisted the bottom of her T-shirt and squeezed out the water. Two ringers in a row. How could she be so lucky?

Ivan had stripped to the waist and had his hands on the snap to his jeans.

Stephanie looked over and felt a rush of panic. Lord, he was getting undressed! Ivan Rasmussen naked. The answer to every woman's dream. This was what she'd wanted, wasn't it? Well, wasn't it?

She swallowed hard and admitted that romance was one thing—naked was another. She might not be ready for naked. Especially since Ivan wasn't inclined to follow through on sexual overtures. What if she got carried away and attacked him, and he rejected her? Good grief, Stephanie, she thought, that's insane. She wasn't going to attack him. The most likely scenario was that she'd start stammering and sweating and probably hyperventilating.

She put her hands on her hips and squinted through the drops of water trickling into her eyes from her soaked bangs. "What are you doing?"

"I'm getting out of my clothes. In case you haven't noticed, they're wet. They're wet because, demented fool that I am, I jumped into the ocean to save you. I don't know why I felt compelled to do that. Lord knows you're perfectly capable of saving yourself. You've been thrown into the Hudson River, probably pushed out of third-story windows, and dragged through rat-infested alleys." He raked his hand through his wet hair. "You know, it's damn hard to be a hero for you."

Stephanie scowled at him. "I don't need a hero."

"What *do* you need?"

She didn't exactly know what she needed. Actually, a hero wouldn't be a bad place to start. A small hero. Nothing on the scale of Superman or Batman. She looked at Ivan. He was heroic enough. Especially now that he was standing in front of her in a pair of tight, soaked-to-the-skin navy blue briefs. He might even be more heroic than she needed, she thought, chewing on her lower lip. "You're going to leave those on, aren't you?" she asked hopefully.

She was nervous. Not much experience with

naked men, he thought. He liked that. He didn't want to share Stephanie with anyone—from her past or present or future. "What happened to being brave?"

Her body responded with a ripple of desire, and her temper flared equally as strongly. "Is this why you dunked me in the water? So you could come in here and flaunt your naked body at me?"

He crossed the room and took a pair of sweats from Ace's bunk. "Just for the record, one more time, I didn't dunk you in the water. You dunked yourself in the water." He knew he was asking for trouble, but he couldn't resist teasing. She was terrific when she was indignant.

"And now that I think about it, I suppose I could make the same accusation. I know you're hot for my body, but this is going to an unnecessary extreme. If you wanted to get me naked—" He turned around just in time to dodge a frying pan.

"Out!" Stephanie shouted, pointing to the hatch. "Out! Out! Out! Before I start throwing knives!"

Ivan stood at midship and watched his passengers depart. He was waiting for Stephanie, wondering if she would warm up when she said good-bye. The atmosphere between them at breakfast had been very frosty, and lunch hadn't been much better. He straightened when he saw Stephanie emerge from the hatch with her backpack slung over one shoulder. She briskly walked past him with her nose tipped up ever so slightly. " 'Bye," Ivan said.

Stephanie narrowed her eyes and threw him a brief sideways glance without breaking stride.

A small smile lit his face. Maybe he'd under-estimated the way she felt about him. She had to have some serious emotions to be so mad. She stormed up the hill without a second glance, and Ivan felt elated at her fury. This is just the beginning, he thought. Winters were long in Maine. It would be nice to have such a challenging project. Stephanie Lowe was doomed.

Mr. and Mrs. Pease approached him. "It was great," Mr. Pease said. "We'll be back next year."

Mrs. Pease looked less enthusiastic. "Next time I'm bringing my heart medicine. That girl with the blue hair and butcher knife sure had me going for a while. And the sea captain's wife just about took my breath away. I don't know how you did it, but darned if it didn't look like a real ghost. I have to tell you, I was pretty startled the first time I saw her standing there on the prow of the ship. But then I knew it was a trick. I figured you did it with movie cameras or something."

Ivan nodded. "Yup. That's exactly how we do it. Movie cameras." He helped Mrs. Pease down the short gangplank and wondered who had put her up to the prank. There were several repeat customers on the voyage, not to mention Ace and Stephanie, all of whom knew about Aunt Tess. Then, of course, there was the other possibility. . . .

Chapter 6

Lucy Pederson had a mop of platinum blond curls. She was a year younger than her cousin Stephanie and an inch shorter—if you didn't count the hair. "No sweat," she said to Stephanie. "I'm going to fix this toilet for you."

"You ever fix a toilet before?"

"No. But if that dunce Stanley could do it, I can do it."

"I still don't see why you couldn't have married him for a little while. Just long enough for him to repair my plumbing. You owed me that!"

Lucy made a disgusted sound and peered into the tank. "I don't know why you're complaining. Most women would cut off a thumb to spend a week with Ivan Rasmussen."

"Yeah, well, if I ever have to spend another week with him, it's not going to be *my* appendage that gets cut off."

Lucy looked at her cousin. "What happened? Did he make a pass at you?"

"I don't know. I thought he did, but then it turned out that he might not have."

"You want to elaborate on that?"

"No."

"You didn't do anything stupid like fall in love with him, did you?"

Stephanie sighed. Of course she'd fallen in love with him. It was like spending four years struggling through a desert with nothing to drink, then coming upon an ice-cream soda.

"Jeez, Stephanie, he's so slippery. Girls have been running after Ivan for as long as I can remember. And he always runs two steps ahead of them." She jiggled something in the tank and screeched when water sprayed up at her. "Shut it off!"

Water splashed against the ceiling and ran down the walls while Stephanie lunged for the shutoff valve.

"You know what I think?" Lucy said, wiping her face on her sleeve. "I think this sucker's broken."

"Doesn't look good," Ivan said, lounging against the doorjamb.

Stephanie jumped at the sound of his voice. "What are you doing here?"

"I have something to discuss with you. Melody was playing her guitar on your widow's walk and shouted down that I should come on in."

Lucy and Stephanie eyed each other.

"I'll go get her," Lucy said.

Ivan looked into the toilet tank. "She's really a sight up there with all that blue hair and her electric guitar. She was the first thing I saw when we sailed into the harbor Saturday."

"She's ruining my inn's image. I wanted it to be dignified, historic, tranquil." Stephanie dropped a bath towel on the floor to sop up the water. "The neighborhood kids are calling her Elvira."

"I think she's just going through a rebellious stage."

"Uh-huh. So what do you think I should do?"

"Lock her up in the cellar until she's forty."

Stephanie squeezed the towel out in the tub and remembered she was supposed to be mad at Ivan. Hell hath no fury like a woman scorned, she thought. That was her—slightly scorned and pretty much humiliated by it all. She wondered how much of her conversation with Lucy he'd heard and gave an involuntary shudder, trying to remember if she'd sounded majorly disappointed at his lack of interest. She stiffened her back and tried to look aloof. "You said you wanted to talk to me?"

"I have a business deal to propose."

A business deal. She'd been hoping for an explanation to soothe her damaged ego, and he had a business deal. Men! She pressed her lips together. "I can hardly wait to get swindled."

Ivan stooped to examine the outside of the toilet bowl. "Last week was the last cruise of the season. The *Savage* won't sail again until spring."

She already knew that. Lucy had moved into Haben last night. She'd given her a free room in exchange for being chief cook and dishwasher. "So?"

"So, I have no place to live. I thought you might rent me a room."

"No!"

Ivan stood and shoved his hands in his pockets. "This toilet is shot. The bowl is cracked beyond repair, and someone's broken the float."

She cocked an eyebrow. "You know about toilets?"

Ivan tried not to smile. "I know enough. I

also know that you're going to have a hard time making ends meet until next summer's tourists flood back to Camden. I'd be willing to pay a nominal amount for a room, and I'd be willing to serve as handyman for the winter."

She needed the money, and she needed a handyman. Did she need Ivan Rasmussen, that was the real question. She needed him like a hole in the head, she decided. Ivan Rasmussen, running hot and cold, underfoot day and night. She might be able to keep her virginity, but she could kiss her sanity good-bye.

"I tell you what. I can sweeten the offer," Ivan said. "You don't have any furniture in this house, and my furniture is sitting unused in storage. If you let me live here, I'll let you use my furniture, free of charge, for an entire year."

Stephanie silently groaned. Ivan had wonderful furniture. Priceless antiques, many of which predated Haben. Mantel clocks, a grandfather clock, pineapple mahogany four-posters, Oriental rugs she would die for, original paintings of all the sea captains and sea captains' wives. The list was endless. "Why do you want to rent a room here? I'd think you'd be anxious to get a place of your own."

"I feel comfortable here, and I'm not sure

what I want to do about a more permanent home for myself."

It was true. His house had been put up for sale so quickly he hadn't had time to consider other arrangements for himself. He'd simply put everything into storage and moved onto the *Savage*. Now that the hectic sailing season was over, he had time to reflect on his actions. It was no wonder Tess was in an uproar, he thought, looking around. Haben had been built to be a Rasmussen house, and she must feel just as displaced as he. He smiled inwardly at the human qualities he'd just given his ancestral ghost. As a kid he'd talked to her all the time. She'd never shown herself to him, but that was to be expected since only women ever saw Tess, and it had never stopped him from carrying on his one-sided conversations.

Stephanie saw his gaze shift to the hall and the window that looked out over the sea and knew she was a goner. For the sake of her wounded pride she told herself it was the grandfather clock that clinched it, but deep down inside she knew the clock was just an excuse. She felt a strong attraction and genuine affection for Ivan. He was hatefully irresistible. He was a teasing scoundrel, and this could prove to be the longest winter of her life. She caught herself gritting her teeth and made a conscious effort to relax.

"Okay," she said, swallowing down a sigh of defeat. "The deal is that I get the use of your furniture for one full year, and you move out June 1. Lucy's doing the cooking, Melody's doing the cleaning, and you're Mr. Fix-it. Now that I have furniture I'll be able to advertise for guests. I don't expect there'll be many, but every little bit helps."

Ivan grinned and checked out his new landlady: tousled brown hair; no makeup, although her cheeks were glowing; sweatshirt with sleeves pushed up to the elbows; and jeans with holes in the knees. She was beautiful, and he was crazy about her. He curled his hand around her neck, pulled her to him, and kissed her hard on the lips.

"I'm used to sleeping in the master bedroom," he said, "and you're going to have to buy a new toilet."

He twirled one of her brown curls around his finger, kissed her on the nose, then seriously on the mouth. Then he sauntered off, down the stairs.

*   *   *

"Oh, gross," Melody said. "A pork chop. Have you ever seen one of these pigs? They're big. I mean *big*. And they feed them chemicals that cause cancer, then they feed them hormones and steroids and antibiotics so that if you eat enough of these chops you get sick and *nothing* can cure you because you have an immunity. And they make them live in filthy little pens with a thousand other pigs, and they pack them into a truck and drive them across the country, so that by the time they get to the packinghouse all their legs are broken. Then they hang them up by their broken hind legs and—"

"I think we get the idea," Ivan said. "How about salad?"

Lucy sliced off a piece of pork chop. "I'd hate for this pig to have died in vain."

Stephanie tenderly pushed her pork chop to one side and poked at her mashed potatoes. "You can't mistreat a potato, can you?"

Melody crunched on a cucumber slice and looked around. "It's nice to eat in the dining room on a real table. Better vibes. The house needed its furniture back."

It was a screwy way to put it, Stephanie thought, but the furniture and the house definitely belonged together. Sounds no longer echoed through hollow rooms. Clocks ticked in soothing cadence. Etchings and oil paintings gave character to blank walls. It had taken only two days to get Ivan and his furniture moved in, and the transformation was amazing. Haben felt like a home. It felt like a haven. It wasn't just the architecture that had given the house its stability. The furniture was an integral part of the building, and as much as Stephanie hated to admit it, so was Ivan.

"How many bottoms do you suppose have sat on this chair?" Melody asked. "Think about it. A hundred years' worth of bottoms. And now my bottom is added to the list. It makes me feel so existential. It makes me feel at one with all the ghosts of bottoms past."

Lucy looked at Stephanie. "All the ghosts of bottoms past?" she repeated. "Excuse me?"

Melody turned her black-rimmed eyes to Ivan. "Tess is happier, too. Boy, was she ticked off at you."

Ivan buttered a herb biscuit. "You've been talking to Tess?"

"I met her on the widow's walk the other day, and we've gotten real tight."

Ivan nodded. "Give her my best."

Stephanie reconsidered her pork chop. She sliced into it, stared at it for a second on the end of her fork, and decided she wasn't hungry after all. "I rented a room today." She took a slip of paper from her shirt pocket and read from it. "Mr. and Mrs. Platz from Lanham, Maryland. Apparently one of the guests on board the *Savage* told them about Haben. They're coming up to see the foliage. They'll be here tomorrow."

Ivan, Melody, and Lucy simultaneously turned to look out the big bay window.

"There isn't any more foliage," Lucy said. "Peak color was last week, and the storm blew all the leaves off the trees."

"Are you sure?" Stephanie had been so busy trying not to think about Ivan that she hadn't had time to think about anything else. She went to the window to take a better look. They were right.

"Well, it's too late now. They're on their way. Besides, it isn't as if we don't have *any* foliage. It's just that the foliage is on the ground, right?" she rationalized. She started to clear the table. "While we've got guests in the house, I'd like everyone to look nice for dinner. Melody, I know this is going to cramp your style, but I'd like your hair to be all one color. And please don't play your electric guitar on the widow's walk. And don't tell them about the pork chops and the pigs' legs getting broken."

Ivan collected plates and followed Stephanie into the kitchen. "Any instructions for me?"

Stephanie gave him a slow, considering look. She had a list of instructions a mile long, and they didn't have anything to do with the guests. They had to do with amorous kisses and sensuous fondlings and the fact that she wasn't getting any. Ivan Rasmussen flirted with her. He watched her every move. And his body language was friendly, very friendly. But he was definitely avoiding a more intimate relationship.

She took the dishes from Ivan and put them in the dishwasher. "No instructions," she said, "but I have a problem with the closet door in my bedroom. It's locked, and I haven't got a key."

Ivan looked puzzled. "How did it get locked? Those closet doors haven't been locked for a hundred years. Nobody has a key."

"Well, somebody has one. I'm telling you, my door is locked."

Ivan took a cookie from the cookie jar. "Let's go take a look at it."

They climbed the wide spiral stairs leading to the second floor and traveled the short hallway, which was now carpeted with a burgundy-and-beige Oriental runner. Stephanie had chosen the smallest of the guest rooms for herself. Melody was living in the maids' quarters in the attic, under the cupola. Lucy and Ivan occupied two other rooms. That left the master bedroom and two adjoining rooms for guests.

Ivan looked in at the master bedroom. "You weren't planning on putting Mr. and Mrs. Platz in there, were you?"

"As a matter of fact, I was. It's our nicest room."

"Aunt Tess isn't going to like having strangers sleeping in her bedroom."

"And I suppose Aunt Tess would prefer to have you in the master bedroom?"

"Absolutely. If you don't believe me, you can ask Melody."

"Melody's credibility is a little shaky in the ghost department. Yesterday she told me Tess wanted chocolate chip cookies."

Ivan stopped in the middle of Stephanie's room, looked at the closed closet door, and looped his arms around Stephanie's waist. "You know what I think? I think you just want me in your bedroom."

Stephanie flinched. That hit home. It hadn't been her motive for bringing him upstairs, but there was enough truth to it to make her uncomfortable. She was becoming more attracted to him with each passing day. And he loved making her uncomfortable, she thought grimly. Rather than ignoring the fact that he'd spurned her advances on board the *Savage*, he continually teased her. The man had a diabolical sense of humor.

Justice really should be served, she decided. Ivan Rasmussen deserved to sweat a little. And all she had to do was turn up the heat. She leaned back in his arms and looked at him. "You're right. I want you in my bedroom. What are you going to do about it?"

There was a flicker of surprise, then his grin widened. "I don't know. Suppose I don't do anything?"

Stephanie moved closer. "Do it my way, or hit the highway, big guy."

"Are you threatening me?"

"You bet. I was at the top of my class in police brutality and sexual harassment. I know how to do things to a man's body that would make your hair stand on end."

"I love it when you talk dirty."

"I wasn't talking dirty!" She punched him lightly in the chest. "This isn't working, is it? Why aren't you getting nervous? You always throw me off-balance. Why can't I get you off-balance?"

His eyes grew serious. "I'm always off-balance. I just hide it better."

"Really?" She wasn't sure if she believed him. Pirates were known to fabricate every now and then.

Ivan noted the skepticism in her voice. She held the winning hand and didn't even know it, he thought. He was in way over his head and sinking fast.

He had his arms around her, and she felt pliant and relaxed now that she was teasing him back. It'd be easy to kiss her, he thought. Her lips were parted in silent laughter and looked soft and inviting. Too tempting to resist. His hand trailed along her neck and the slope of her shoulder, and his mouth took hers

Stephanie had expected to be kissed, but she hadn't counted on this sort of kiss. She'd expected the kiss to be impudent, like the bathroom kiss two days ago. The bathroom kiss had been a pirate's kiss—infuriating but fun. Exactly what you'd expect from a charming rat. The kiss they were sharing now was fragile. It was a serious kiss, more demanding in an entirely new way—and much more confusing. Stephanie pulled away and looked into Ivan's eyes, not sure of what she saw there.

Pay attention, Stephanie, Ivan thought. This is love. He kissed her again, pulling her in deeper, persuading her to respond to him. "Are you still off-balance?" he asked.

"More than ever."

"Good. I hate being the only one who feels insecure and desperate."

Ivan Rasmussen? Insecure? And then it hit her. He wasn't going so slowly because he wasn't interested in her. He was going slowly because he cared about her. Really cared. He didn't want to rush things. Didn't want to lessen their relationship by pressing the physical aspect of it. A smile surfaced.

"I think I've been dumb," Stephanie said. "You like me, don't you?"

Like her? Ivan groaned. She was his reason for getting up in the morning. She was the sun, and he felt himself revolving around her, held tight by some mysterious, overwhelming force that was much more inescapable than mere gravity. "Yeah. I like you." His voice was husky. "I like you a lot."

"I like you, too," Stephanie said. She ran the flat of her palm across his chest, enjoying the feel of hard muscle and warm flesh beneath his shirt. Her fingertip stroked up the side of his neck and along the line of his bearded jaw. She wasn't sure of his ultimate intentions, but she knew he'd shown her a part of himself that was very private. And she knew from the pressure against his zipper that the intimate web he'd woven around them was fueling more aggressive desires in him. He was a pirate after all, she thought happily. And he was making love to her, seducing her slowly and thoroughly.

"This is special, isn't it?" she asked, winding her arms around his neck and sensuously brushing her lips across his. She felt his hand tighten at the small of her back, felt him stir when she pressed her hips forward.

She was taunting him, Ivan thought. She finally recognized her power. She was making him burn with each erotic movement of her body. She was telling him that she wanted him. And Lord knew, he wanted her.

"I'm probably making a mistake by not locking the bedroom door right now," he said, "but I think we should put this on hold. I don't want to make love to you, then discover Lucy and Melody have been listening on the other side of the door."

"Speaking of doors—the closet is definitely locked."

Ivan turned and tugged, but the door wouldn't open. "Wait here. There's a big old skeleton key in the master bedroom that might work."

He returned a couple of moments later, tried the key, and gave Stephanie a wink when the lock tumbled. He swung the door open with a flourish, and a cadaver fell out, crashing onto the floor at Stephanie's feet.

Stephanie made a strangled sound and clamped her hand over her mouth.

Ivan hung on to the door and took a deep breath to steady his heart. "Jeez!"

Both took a step back from the body.

"This guy's been embalmed!" Ivan said. "He's wearing makeup."

"Looks to be in his seventies," Stephanie said. "This is sick. This is really sick!"

Stephanie reached out for Ivan with a

shaky hand. "You know what's even sicker? Me. I hate to be a wimp about this, but I think I'm going to throw up. Yes, I'm definitely going to throw up," she said, rushing to the bathroom.

Five minutes later, she was seated on the tile floor, resting her back against the tub with a wet towel draped over her head.

Ivan massaged her shoulders. "You feel better?"

Stephanie nodded. "This is embarrassing."

"I thought cops got used to seeing stiffs."

"I was in narcotics, not homicide, and believe it or not, I've never had a dead person fall out of a closet at me."

"I hope you're not going to blame this on Aunt Tess."

"Ivan, your house is a loony bin."

"Honey, this is *your* house."

She removed the towel and pushed herself to her feet. "We should call the police. Some undertaker is going nuts looking for that poor old man."

They walked down the hall to her bedroom and stopped at the door, not able to believe their eyes. The body was gone.

"Am I imagining this?" Stephanie asked.

"Did I just throw up over a figment of my imagination?"

"I can guarantee you he didn't walk away."

"So someone took the dead guy. While I was in the bathroom, someone came in here and bodynapped him."

They exchanged glances and knew they were both thinking the same thing. "Melody!" they called in unison.

Melody came to the head of the stairs. "What do you want?"

"There was a dead body here, and now it's gone. I don't suppose you know anything about this?"

Melody looked interested. "A dead body? A grossly dead body?"

Stephanie furiously pushed her damp hair back from her forehead, feeling herself teetering on the edge of civility. She'd tried to be philosophical about the toilet, the porch, the water heater, and the multitude of bizarre things that had happened to her, but this was the end. Disappearing bodies were not part of the bargain.

She glared at Melody. "Someone took that body. That body did not just up and walk away. Even Ivan said so. Someone took it, and there's only one person in this house who would be nutso enough to do it. You. I know you took that body. Now where is it?"

"She's getting a little weird," Melody said to Ivan. "Probably PMS."

Lucy came up behind Melody. "What's all the racket about?"

"They think I took a body," Melody said. "They're missing one."

Lucy looked from Melody to Stephanie to Ivan. "Uh-huh."

"It's true," Stephanie said to Lucy. "There was a body here." She lifted the dust ruffle and looked under her bed. "My closet door was locked, so Ivan came up to unlock it, and this dead guy fell out at me, and I threw up, and then *poof*, the body is missing."

Lucy looked doubtful. "You're putting me on, right?"

"No." Ivan sat on the edge of the bed. "That actually happened . . . I think."

"And they think I took it." Melody rolled her huge black-rimmed eyes. "What do I look like, a body snatcher?"

"This body, did it have a knife sticking in it? Was there a bullet hole in the forehead? A rope tied around the neck?" Lucy asked.

"No. It was an old guy in a gray suit with a maroon tie," Stephanie told her. "He was fine, except he was dead, and he should have had a different tie. Maybe something with stripes."

"Why do you think Melody took him?"

Stephanie looked under the bed one more time. "It seemed like something Melody would do."

"Mmmm, that's true. But Melody was with me, cleaning the kitchen."

Melody's eyes looked even wider than usual. "Are you going to call the police?"

Stephanie flipped her palms up. "I don't know what I'd say to them. Some refugee from a funeral home fell out of my closet, then disappeared while I was throwing up? They'd give me a breathalizer."

Ivan took Stephanie by the hand. "Come on. We're going to check out this entire house, then we're going to have dessert."

Two hours later Ivan and Stephanie sat in the kitchen, eating ice-cream sundaes.

"This is very creepy," Stephanie said. "This is one of the creepiest things that's ever happened to me."

"Coming from you, that's quite a statement."

Stephanie spooned more fudge sauce over

her ice cream. "Being a narc wasn't usually creepy. It was boring, dangerous, scary, and frustrating. Mostly frustrating."

Ivan was curious about her past. It didn't have anything to do with the fact that she'd been a cop. If she'd been a secretary or a second-grade teacher, he would have been equally curious. He simply wanted to know about Stephanie. "Why did you become a cop? Can you talk about it?"

"Yeah, the beginning is easy to talk about. It's the end that's tough."

She mashed her ice cream into mush. "I was in college, majoring in art for lack of something better. Lots of kids go to college and have this passion to learn or to go out into the world and be a doctor, or a CPA, or an astronaut. I didn't have a passion for anything. I was just drifting through life. I was an average person, getting average grades, going to college because that was the average thing to do. Then one day my mom called and said my little brother was in the hospital from a drug overdose. My little brother!" She shook her head, still wondering how such a thing could have happened.

"He was a good kid. We lived in a decent neighborhood. It just blew my mind. There I was, marking time in college as if I were some zombie, and my brother was lying in a hospital bed, fighting for his life. My brother got over it, but I never did. I decided I wanted to do something about the drugs in my neighborhood, so I quit college and became a cop."

"Any regrets about leaving college?"

She scraped the bottom of her sundae glass. "No. College just wasn't for me."

"Any regrets about buying my house?"

Stephanie laughed. "Lots!"

Ivan tapped his spoon against the rim of his glass. "There's something strange going on here, Steph. Someone cracked that upstairs toilet. And someone purposely weakened the boards in the front porch. And someone put a corpse in your closet."

"You think someone's out to get me?"

"Someone is trying to make your life difficult here. You think someone from New Jersey followed you? Someone with a vendetta?"

She snorted. "If someone from New Jersey was after me, I'd have a bullet in my head. At the very least they'd burn the house to the ground."

"How about someone local?"

"I don't know many people. You'd be my

only suspect. This house was in your family for generations. Maybe you want it back—at a lowered price."

He slouched in his chair. "Sorry, it's not me. I'm broke. I couldn't buy it back at any price."

Stephanie watched him, waiting for an explanation, but he didn't offer any. How could he be broke? He'd just sold a house that probably didn't even have a mortgage on it. He had a successful cruise business. He wasn't supporting a wife and kids.

He stood and took his glass to the dishwasher. "You know, it really bothers me that we couldn't find the corpse. Melody and Lucy were in the kitchen. You and I were in the bathroom. And in the space of ten minutes, someone got that body out of the house."

Stephanie agreed. "There's something else that bothers me. Whoever locked the body in my closet knew about the skeleton key. Do you have any secret passages in this house? Any long-lost deranged relatives living in concealed rooms?"

"You've been watching too many movies."

She pushed back in her chair. "Lucy called every mortuary within a forty-mile radius, and no one was missing an old man in a gray suit.

I can't believe we've hit a dead end on this. What have we overlooked?"

He pulled her to her feet and hooked his arm around her waist. "And you thought Maine was going to be dull." He nestled her against him, pleased at the feel of her in his arms.

"Tell me the truth, do you mind that I've turned Haben into a bed-and-breakfast inn?"

A small, tight, humorless smile curved his mouth. "You think I'm behind all of this, don't you?"

Stephanie smiled back at him—a broad, brash, teasing smile. "Let's just say you're not above suspicion."

Chapter 7

Eileen Platz was a small woman in her early fifties. She was rail thin with short jet-black hair and sharp, dark eyes. Her husband had the large frame of an athlete and the soft paunch of a man gone sedentary. They stood on Haben's newly reconstructed front porch and looked at the ground, which was covered with leaves, then looked at the bare trees and briefly exchanged glares.

"I told you we should have come last week," Eileen Platz said, her mouth pressed into a mean little line.

"Don't start, Eileen. It wasn't my idea to drive fourteen hours to see a bunch of dying leaves."

Lucy watched them from the front window. "What do you think? Do you think we should let them slug it out, or should we invite them in?"

"I need the money," Stephanie told her. "Let's haul them in here and feed them some sparkling cider and crackers and cheese." She opened the door, introduced herself, and was pleased to see their attitude change once they were inside the house.

"This is lovely," Eileen Platz said. "This is like living in a museum. It's absolutely beautiful."

"Eileen's a big history buff," her husband explained. "And she's a real antique hound."

"Then I'm sure you'll enjoy Haben." Stephanie gave them a room key and directed them to the master bedroom. "When you're settled in, you can come downstairs for cheese and cider."

Melody swept into the foyer and stopped short at coming face-to-face with Mr. and Mrs. Platz. She was dressed entirely in black: short black boots, black tights, short black skirt, black leather jacket, and big, dangly black earrings. Her face was pancake white with her usual raccoon eye makeup, and her hair was brilliant orange.

Stephanie stifled a gasp at the orange hair and reminded herself that she'd only asked Melody to make her hair all one color. Probably she should be more specific after this. Probably

Melody thought this would be appropriate since Halloween was coming up.

"Melody, this is Mr. and Mrs. Platz. They're going to be staying in the master bedroom. Would you mind helping them with their bags?"

"No sweat. Just call me Cinderella." She hefted a suitcase and smiled at Mrs. Platz. "I like your hair. Is that Clairol Ebony? I had my hair that color in March."

Stephanie turned to Ivan. "Maybe I'm not cut out for this. I have a nagging premonition of disaster."

"You'll get used to it. This is a lot like running a schooner. For the most part, it's fun. You get to meet a lot of new people, and you get to share a part of the past with them."

"Mmmm, but you never had Melody for a bellhop."

"No. I was blessed with Ace."

Stephanie grinned. "I guess we each have our own cross to bear. You never answered my question last night. Does it bother you to see Haben turned into an inn?"

He slung his arm around her shoulders. It didn't bother him to see Haben turned into an inn, but he wasn't sure about turning Stephanie

153

into an innkeeper. He'd rather see her turned into a wife and mother. Selfish attitude, he told himself. There wasn't any reason why she couldn't be wife, mother, *and* innkeeper. This was the twentieth-first century. Women wore many hats.

Ivan sighed. Right now, he didn't care about Stephanie's hats. At this particular moment he was more interested in her lingerie. He wondered if that made him a sexist oaf. Probably. Probably he should drag his mind out of the bedroom and keep it in the foyer for a while.

He pushed away all thoughts of lingerie and forced himself to concentrate on her question. "I think it's a great idea. If I'd kept Haben, I might have done the same. Mrs. Platz is right. This is like a museum. It'd be a shame not to share it."

"I know I'm prying, but why did you sell?"

He shrugged. "I needed the money. I offered the house to relatives first, but no one wanted to buy it. It's big and expensive to maintain."

"It must have been difficult for you to part with Haben."

Ivan nodded. "Sometimes you don't fully appreciate something until you've lost it. I have to admit, while I was living here, I considered it to be something of an albatross."

"Have you always lived in this house?"

He shook his head. "I did when I was a kid, but after I graduated from high school, I went away to college. Then, when I quit college, I got my own apartment. Actually, apartment is glorifying it. What I had was a room over Gerty's Bait Shop."

"Why did you quit college?"

"I was in my junior year when my grandfather died and left me the *Savage*. It was just a forgotten wreck of a ship, dying a slow death in Nantucket, but he owned it, and he willed it to me. As soon as I saw it, I was in love. I was a lot like you. I really didn't know why I was in college, except that was what had been expected of me. Anyway, I quit school and got a job on a trawler to pay for the restoration. Most of it I did myself.

"Two years ago my mother died, and last year my dad died. I gave up my room over Gerty's and moved back into Haben while I straightened out the estate. I love this house, but it's much too big for a bachelor. It was built to hold lots of noisy people. It needs to have kids running around in it, and dogs barking, and it needs a big orange cat curled up in the Queen Anne wing chair."

"You could have managed that. All you had to do was find a wife."

"Seemed like a high price to pay for noise."

Stephanie wondered at the pain that statement caused her. "Mmmm. I suppose pirates aren't very domestic."

Ivan tugged her closer. "Doesn't have anything to do with being domestic. It has to do with finding the right woman."

"Picky, are you?"

"Very. Marriage isn't something a person should rush into."

Stephanie stared at him for a moment. "I can't imagine you rushing into marriage."

He'd choose very carefully, and his marriage would last forever, she thought. If the family photos and paintings on the wall were any indication, he came from a long line of family-oriented Rasmussens. Again, there was the twinge of pain that she preferred not to analyze.

She decided to steer the conversation in a lighter direction, so she wrinkled her nose and teased him. "You seem more like the sort to be dragged to the altar—kicking and screaming."

Ivan stared back at her. He'd always thought

so, too. He'd liked his easy bachelor existence. It was amazing how something ridiculous, such as a broken toilet, could change your entire outlook on life. All his plans for the future now included Stephanie. Bachelordom had become a colossal bore.

There was the sound of tires screeching outside the house, and Ivan and Stephanie ran to the window in time to see a car swerve onto the sidewalk and come to a bumpy stop with two wheels on the curb. Its driver rested his head on the steering wheel for a second, took a disbelieving look at Haben, and shook his forehead before slowly driving away.

"Melody must be up on the widow's walk again," Stephanie said. She stormed outside and looked up at Melody. "What are you doing up there? You're a traffic hazard."

"I'm talking to Tess. She doesn't like Mrs. Platz being in her bedroom. She says she doesn't mind making this into an inn, but she doesn't want strangers in her bedroom. Oh yeah, and she wants pineapple upside-down cake for dessert tonight."

Ivan made sure the doors were locked and the windows secure. Stephanie shut off the lights and took the hand Ivan offered when he met her in the foyer.

"So, lady innkeeper, what do you think of this hotel business?"

"I think it will be fun. What do you think?"

Ivan smiled wanly. "I think it will be a pain in the butt. I spent the entire evening explaining household artifacts to Mrs. Platz. What I really wanted to do was find a dark corner and make out with you."

Stephanie looked at him. "Do grown-ups make out?"

"Yeah. When grown-ups do it they call it foreplay. And it's pretty hot stuff."

"And Mrs. Platz made me miss it. Will there be another opportunity?"

His hands splayed across her back, and his mouth met hers in a slow, sensuous kiss. "You can't escape it." His lips moved to her temple, then her ear, and he told her some of the details of foreplay.

Stephanie got a rush that went from her heart to her doodah. He was right. It was pretty hot stuff. She rocked back on her heels when he released her. "Wow."

"Play your cards right, and tomorrow I might tell you more. I might even demonstrate."

"Promises, promises."

A promise he was going to enjoy keeping. In fact, he'd like to keep it later in the night. Or even better, he'd like to keep it *now*. It could take months for her to really learn to love him, he reasoned. He didn't think he could wait months. Maybe he was being greedy. Maybe he should be content with being liked a lot. She already liked him a lot. And he really shouldn't hold off because of her virginity. That would be discrimination. He didn't want to be accused of being a sexual bigot. He almost had himself convinced when the phone rang.

"I have to get this," Stephanie said, moving out of his arms. "It's probably my mother. She always waits for the rates to go down before calling."

Her mother. It might as well have been a call from God. So much for rationalization. He waved good night and went upstairs, telling himself it was all for the best, but not quite believing it. He had payroll checks to sign and a stack of ledgers to go over. Pretty boring stuff compared to relieving Stephanie of her virginity.

Half an hour later Stephanie crept up the stairs and got undressed in the privacy of her room. She dropped a warm nightgown over her head, checked her closet, and looked under her bed before creeping under the big down quilt. The wind had picked up since the afternoon, whistling in the eaves and roaring through the oak tree just outside her window. She was glad she'd had Ivan remove the screens and put the storm windows in place. The heating bill was going to be prohibitive if they had this much wind throughout the winter.

She switched off her bedside light and was thankful for the quiet. Obviously Eileen Platz hadn't found any dead people in her closet. There would have been a scream by now. She wondered if Lucy and Melody were having trouble sleeping. Probably not. They hadn't seemed too upset about the corpse. Of course, they hadn't seen him. He hadn't crashed down onto *their* feet. She closed her eyes and tried to relax, but there were too many things rolling through her mind—mostly thoughts of Ivan.

She slid out of bed, temporarily giving up on sleep, and went to the window. She'd chosen this bedroom because, like the master bedroom, it was at the back of the house and overlooked the harbor. She raised the shade and pulled the sheer curtain aside. It was a dark night, but she could see the outlines of the tall ships against the black water. One of them was the *Savage*, she thought, feeling a surge of pride and affection.

She slumped onto the chintz-covered window seat and looked into the night with unfocused eyes. She wondered if Ivan was already asleep in the bedroom across the hall and felt a vague discontent that they were separated. They weren't married or engaged. They weren't even lovers. There was no justification for the loneliness and frustration she felt, but she felt it all the same. Some of it was sexual. As Ace would put it, she was a hotbed of raging hormones. Thanks to Ivan Rasmussen.

She was musing about the pleasures of love when a gust of wind shook the house, and the dead man in the gray suit swung past her window.

It happened so fast, Stephanie thought she'd imagined it. When he swung by a second time, she stifled a scream and jumped from the window seat in astonishment. It took a moment for her to gather her wits and shake away the initial horror. There was an explanation for this, and she was going to find out what it was.

She moved toward the window when another blast of wind buffeted Haben, and the dead man crashed through the window, feet-first. His eyes were closed in eternal slumber, and his hands were innocently clasped across his chest. He smashed into the wooden window frame, and his feet flew up from the impact, almost kicking Stephanie in the head.

She instinctively jumped back, losing her balance and sprawling on the rug amid a shower of broken glass. By the time she'd scrambled to her feet, the man was gone. She stood helpless, inches from the window seat, afraid to move in her bare feet.

"Ivan!"

He was at her door even before she'd called. "What was that crash?" He looked at the window and at the glass surrounding her.

"It was the guy in the suit," Stephanie said. "He was flying around past my window. Next thing I knew, he'd crashed right through. Never moved a muscle. Had his eyes closed the whole time."

Ivan grimaced. "Steph, the man's been embalmed. You didn't expect him to open his eyes and say howdy, did you?"

"No, but then I didn't expect him to crash through my window either."

He walked across the room and looked out the window. He scooped Stephanie into his arms and crunched over the glass shards to the door. "Stay here," he said, setting her on her feet. "Don't move from this spot. I'm going outside to investigate, and I don't want you running around the house in your nightgown."

Five minutes later he was back. "I couldn't find anything. I'm calling the police."

Stephanie grabbed him by the shirtfront. "No! You can't do that. No one will ever stay here again. What am I going to say to Eileen Platz? She's not going to understand about some old guy in a gray suit turning up in closets and crashing through windows. It'll get in the newspapers. They'll say the house is possessed. I'm in enough freakin' trouble with Melody up there on the widow's walk."

The line of his mouth tightened. "Okay, but you can't sleep here, and I'm not leaving you alone. This dead guy has a definite preference for your room."

He hooked his hand behind her knees and lifted her into his arms. He quietly closed the door and carried her across the hall. "You can stay with me tonight." It was a sign, he decided, his tongue firmly planted in his cheek—and much more potent than a phone call from her mother. It would be wrong to ignore a definite sign such as this. "We could see if tab A fits into slot B."

"Are you kidding me? How can you think of tabs and slots at a time like this? There's a dead guy running around out there! And why are you dressed? You don't even have your shoes off."

"I had business to attend to." Shoe factory business, he thought with distaste. I wasn't cut out for the shoe business. Hopefully, sometime soon he could close that chapter of his life. He kissed her lightly on the lips. "And you're still suspicious of me, aren't you?"

"I don't know. I think my nerves are shot. Too many years of being a cop. Too many days of living with Melody."

He pulled her into his room and locked the door. "You need to relax," he said, smiling wolfishly. And *he* needed to relax. He hadn't had a decent night's sleep since he'd met her.

Relax? In his bedroom? In her nightgown? She couldn't remember feeling more *unre-laxed*. It was funny how just moments ago when she was all alone, she'd thought it would be comfy to spend the night next to Ivan Rasmussen, and now that it was a definite possibility, she felt like jumping out the window.

He had his hands at her hip, and his eyes gazed into hers, seeing the mirror image of his own excitement and his own apprehension. In all seriousness, he'd intended to wait a while longer before making love to her, but there was no way he was going to leave her alone and unprotected—and he knew there was no way he could spend the night with her and not make love. He rubbed his thumb over her panty elastic, enjoying the simple intimacy, and moved his hands up her sides to frame her breasts. He felt her shiver at his touch and saw her face light with pleasure.

"I like this nightgown," he said, his voice soft and seductive. "It's sexy, with its high, ruffled neck and long, ruffled sleeves. It covers you from head to foot, but it clings in all the right places."

She stood absolutely still, barely breathing as he pulled the thin translucent material taut over her breasts. He lowered his mouth and kissed her, slowly, and her doodah started to hum a little tune.

Doodah humming aside, there was no doubt in her mind that being with Ivan was right. She'd known Steve for years and hadn't known him at all, and she'd known Ivan for a very short time and felt as if she knew all that was important about him.

There had been an overwhelming chemistry between them from the very beginning, but that wouldn't have been enough. It was enough for kisses and a few fantasies, but it wasn't enough to make her want to spend the night next to him. She realized now that she had to love a man to think of doing that. Ivan was very close and very real, and she loved him.

She tugged his shirttails from the waistband of his jeans and slid her palms along the flat plane of his stomach and the hard wall of his chest. "I'm glad I waited all these years," she said. "I'm glad my first time is with you."

"Hmmm, so do you love me?" he asked, flicking the overhead light off, unbuttoning his shirt. "How much?"

Stephanie smiled at him. "Enough."

"Enough for what?"

"Enough for anything you have in mind."

Ivan's grin flashed white in the subdued light

of the bedroom. He kicked his shoes off and nestled her close to him. He kissed her temple and the sensitive spot just below her ear.

He wanted to go slow, to make it beautiful for her, but she was making control difficult, and he felt a rush of heat slam into him as her hands explored the small of his back and slid below his waistband.

He groaned and moved against her, kissing her hard. The kiss deepened, demanded more, promised everything. He laid her on the bed, inching her nightgown over her head, moving the material slowly, kissing each new inch of exposed flesh—the inside of her knee, her thigh, dark slick shadows, and all the soft feminine places pirates like him loved to ravish. He watched her arch under his kisses, her breathing shallow, her eyes following his every move.

"Steph, are you sure? We could stop here . . ." Not easily, he thought, but he could manage it.

"I'm sure."

Lord, how he loved her. The strength of it almost took his breath away. He was taking something very special from her, and he wanted to make sure he was replacing it with something equally wonderful. In his heart he offered her everything he valued—fidelity, trust, respect, affection, passion.

"I love you," he whispered, his hand sliding across her belly, dipping lower, stroking, inflaming.

She whispered the words back. "I love *you*." And she really did love him, she thought. And she loved what he was doing to her.

"Do you like this?" he asked, his finger circling the center of her universe.

"Yes," she said on a sigh.

And then it happened . . . her universe exploded.

It was dark when she awoke. The wind had slowed and rain pelted the windowpane. It was a good thing Ivan had gone back to her room to tack plastic over the broken window. After he'd secured the plastic they'd showered together and made love again—for a very long time. They'd talked in hushed voices, enjoying the easy intimacy their loving had brought. They'd teased and explored and found preferences, finally losing themselves to the desire they'd created, and they'd fallen asleep with legs and arms entwined. It had been the nicest possible night, she thought. If it had followed an elaborate white-gowned ceremony, it couldn't have been any more perfect.

She snuggled closer and swept her hand the length of him, almost as a reassurance that he was real. He stirred in his sleep and wrapped his arms around her, his touch renewing the now familiar pulse of desire.

Ivan wasn't sure if he was dreaming or if he was awake—and didn't care. He rolled over, and in one smooth, swift movement made her gasp at the speed of his reaction, leaving no doubt in her mind that he was the direct descendant of a pirate.

Stephanie mustered her reserves and gingerly eased herself onto a chair at the breakfast table.

Ivan looked up from his plate of pancakes and couldn't resist teasing. "Have a rough night?"

She glanced over her shoulder to make sure the dining room was empty. "Why am I the only one walking funny?"

"Because you're the one who got greedy and woke me up in the middle of the night," he said, covering her hand with his and smiling at her with such unabashed affection that she was sure anyone watching would instantly know they'd shared a bed.

"Don't men get sore?"

"I try to keep in shape," he bragged, polishing off a tumbler of fresh-squeezed orange juice. "Practice, practice, practice."

Mr. and Mrs. Platz came in and took seats at the table. "It's raining," Mrs. Platz said morosely. "First no leaves, and now rain. And this is a lovely inn, but I hardly slept last night. The wind was howling, something terrible. And there were thumping noises and crashing noises. Lord, for a while there it sounded as if something was banging on my window."

Melody served them pancakes and sausage and glasses of juice. "Must have been Tess. I warned you about putting Mr. and Mrs. Platz in that room."

Eileen Platz put her hand to her throat. "Who's Tess?"

"Tess is our ghost," Melody told her cheerfully. "She's really a nice old lady, but she only likes to have Ivan sleep in her bedroom."

"Well," Mrs. Platz said, sizing up Ivan, "I don't suppose I blame her."

Ivan tipped back in his chair. "Tess was the wife of Red Rasmussen, the pirate. She predates this house by about 150 years, but the current Haben was built directly over the foundation of the original Haben, and some believe she's taken up residence here. Legend has it that Red died at sea, and Tess died waiting for him."

"How romantic," Mrs. Platz said. "How sad."

"It wasn't Tess that was at the window last night," Stephanie said. "It was—" She paused and poured herself a cup of coffee. "It was the wind. It blew one of the branches from the oak tree into my window and smashed the glass. We're going to have to trim that tree back," she added lamely, looking at Ivan.

Mr. Platz dug into the sausages. "These are terrific. Are they homemade?"

"I get them from the butcher down the street," Stephanie said. "He makes fresh sausage every Thursday."

Melody brought herself a plate of pancakes and took her place at the table. She eyed the sausage critically.

"Does he add nitrates? Is the meat cured?" She opened her dark eyes extra wide. "I read about nitrates. They're chemicals that they put in the meat to make it change color and stuff, and they give you cancer. They make your pancreas rot away, and you die writhing in pain.

171

And if you drink beer while you eat the nitrates, you get huge cancerous tumors that grow all over your body. And do you know what they make sausage out of? Ground-up pigs. Have you ever seen a sausage pig? They're big. We're talking really *big*—"

"Excuse me," Stephanie said, "I think we've already had the discussion about pigs."

Melody blinked black mascara-caked lashes at her. "Oh, yeah. Sorry."

Mrs. Platz leaned forward. "About this ghost, has anyone ever seen her?"

"I talk to her all the time," Melody said. She lowered her voice for emphasis. "We be mates."

Mrs. Platz's eyes glittered, and she sucked air through her narrow mouth. "Do you think she'd talk to me? I've always felt very strong cosmic vibrations, but I've never actually talked to a ghost."

Melody shrugged. "She hangs out on the widow's walk."

"Does she materialize? Does she drip ectoplasm?"

Melody's face was expressionless as she ate her pancakes. "Mostly she just hangs out."

"Well, how do you contact her? Do you

have to go into a trance? Do you need a white candle?"

"She likes cookies," Melody said. "She has a real sweet tooth."

Mrs. Platz looked confused. "How can a ghost eat cookies?"

"I eat them," Melody said matter-of-factly. "Then I tell her about them, and she gets turned on by that."

"Lord, I would *love* to see a ghost. My neighbor, Sophia Schroth, would die if she knew I'd talked to a ghost." She looked at her husband. "I knew I should have gone to the window last night."

"Ms. Lowe said it was the wind, and that's what it was . . . the wind," Mr. Platz told her.

"It was the wind at Ms. Lowe's window, but it might have been Tess at ours. We were sleeping in her bedroom."

Mr. Platz rolled his eyes. "You need to get help, Eileen. You're beginning to sound like your aunt Rose." Mr. Platz leaned toward Ivan and spoke in a confidential voice. "Her aunt Rose talks to Walter Cronkite all day."

Mrs. Platz pinched her lips together. "I believe in ghosts. I always have, and I always will. And I can feel that there's a ghost in this house."

"Hah! Some ghost," Mr. Platz said. "Has to knock on windows to get into her own bedroom. If she's such a hot ghost, why doesn't she just waltz through the wall? Any self-respecting ghost can waltz through walls."

Mrs. Platz dismissed him with a wave of her hand. "Don't pay any attention to him," she said to Melody. "He doesn't understand about these things. He has no psychic energy."

Melody poured more maple syrup on her pancakes and nodded in understanding.

"Do you think if I went up to the widow's walk, I would get to see her?" Mrs. Platz asked Melody. "Do you suppose you could introduce me?"

"Sure. Hey, anybody who uses Clairol Ebony's okay in my book."

Mr. Platz grunted. "You think she'll be out in the rain? Won't her ectoplasm get wet?"

"I don't know," Melody said. "But she grooves on fog."

Stephanie kept her eyes averted and concentrated on her mashed potatoes. She felt hideously sorry for Eileen Platz, and at the same time was on the verge of bursting out laughing. The poor woman had maintained a marathon vigil with nothing to show for it other than a red nose and frozen feet. At one point a small crowd had even gathered to watch the two crazy women standing in the rain on the top of Haben. The local cable station had sent a minicam, and a kid from the high school paper had stopped by to get details. The astonishing part was that everyone seemed to know about Tess, and no one disputed her existence. What the people of Camden, Maine, couldn't understand was why Eileen Platz thought it necessary to talk to old Red's widow. Stephanie chewed a piece of fried chicken and wondered about the sanity of New Englanders.

Melody looked as if she'd fared considerably better than Mrs. Platz. Her hair was freshly washed and starched and more brilliantly orange than ever. "It's a shame you didn't get to see Tess," she said to Mrs. Platz. "She probably went to the mall."

Eileen Platz sat a little stiffer in her chair, and Stephanie thought she was most likely trying to decide if she'd been made a fool of. She couldn't begin to guess why Mrs. Platz had believed Melody in the first place. Because you believe what you want to believe, she told herself. Eileen Platz wanted to believe there was a ghost on the widow's walk. Just like all those kids in the rehab programs had wanted to believe drugs would help them cope, make them smarter, make them cool, make them sexier, give them energy. She almost wished Mrs. Platz had seen Tess. After standing in the rain for seven hours, Mrs. Platz deserved to see *something*.

"Cheer up," Mr. Platz said to his wife. "We're staying here one more night. Maybe the ghost will come back and knock on your window some more."

Chapter 8

Stephanie pulled down the shade on her brand-new window and turned to look at the man sprawled on her bed, taking in his gray wool socks, lean muscular legs encased in soft faded jeans, awesome bulge behind his zipper, unbuttoned shirt displaying a swath of hard, smooth chest and stomach. His hair needs cutting, and his beard should be bronzed, Stephanie thought. She'd never thought of a beard as being an instrument of torture, but Ivan knew how to exact a price with his. "Do you think Mrs. Platz will make contact with Tess tonight?"

Ivan grinned. "It's possible. Tess should be back from the mall by now."

"You know, this is crazy, but I'm beginning to feel as if I actually live with Tess. I think I know how Jimmy Stewart felt about Harvey."

He put a pillow behind his head and motioned for her to come to him. He liked being friends with Stephanie. He'd like to lie there and talk, he thought, but already the pressure was building in him, and he knew talk would be put aside for a while. It was early, barely ten o'clock, but he didn't know how he'd lasted this long. His worst fears for the bed-and-breakfast business were coming true. It was almost impossible to get Stephanie alone.

When they were married—and there was no doubt in his mind that they'd be married—she could run the inn during the summer months, if she wanted. In the winter, he'd like the house to be theirs. He didn't want to share Stephanie year-round with a constant flow of guests.

She smiled slyly and crawled onto the bed, reminding him of a predatory feline, and straddled him at the hips. It hasn't taken her long to assert her sexuality, he thought, pleased. She wasn't afraid to say what she liked, and she wasn't afraid to be aggressive. Those were traits that followed her in and out of the bedroom. Strength. She had strength of character. He slid his hands under her gray Rutgers University sweatshirt and confirmed what he'd suspected. No bra.

She'd seemed surprised when he'd strolled into her bedroom five minutes before and kicked his shoes off. She'd thought about it for a moment and lowered the shade. She hadn't questioned his moving in, and he hadn't asked permission. He was probably being presumptuous as hell, he thought, but it felt natural. Besides, there was the dead guy in the gray suit. Ivan didn't care how many years of karate she'd had, he didn't care if she had a marksman rating, and he didn't care how many times she'd survived being thrown into the Hudson River. He had no intention of letting her sleep alone until he found out what was going on in Haben.

She leaned back slightly, popped the snap to his jeans, and slowly slid the zipper all the way down. His hands grasped her at the waist. "Pretty brazen," he said, with a smile.

"I was afraid you were going to strangle."

The room was lit by a small ginger jar table lamp that sat on her nightstand. It was a small room, one of the few in the house that Stephanie had filled with her own furniture. She stood at the side of the brass bed and peeled her shirt over her head, enjoying the way he watched her with affection and desire and a touch of amusement. Because there was the hint of a smile playing at the corners of his mouth, she smiled, too. "You like being entertained, don't you?"

Ivan reached out for her, but she stepped away. She unzipped her jeans and worked them down her legs in a sensuous slow motion that caused her breasts to sway seductively. She came a little closer and stuck her thumb in the elastic waist of her bikini panties.

"I didn't think virgins were allowed to wear panties like that," Ivan said.

"I'm not a virgin anymore. I bought these panties five years ago, and I've been saving them for this special occasion."

He removed his shirt and shucked his own jeans. "They're very pretty, but if you value them, you'd better get them off. I've got about thirty seconds of self-control left, and then I'm going to rip those panties to shreds."

Stephanie was half-asleep when she heard Eileen Platz shouting. She sprang out of bed and had her hand on the doorknob when she realized she was naked. She grabbed a terry-cloth robe, belted it quickly, and ran into the hall. She was almost knocked over by Mrs. Platz, rushing from the master bedroom.

"It was there!" Mrs. Platz screamed. "It was at my window. The ghost!"

Lucy and Melody joined them. "What's going on?"

Mr. Platz staggered from the bedroom. He pointed to the window, opened his mouth, and crashed to the floor.

Stephanie bent over him. "He's fainted. Lucy, get me a wet cloth."

Mr. Platz opened his eyes. "Did I faint? It was awful. It was horrible. I'm going home to Maryland right now, and I'm never coming back." He struggled to his feet. "That Tess is the ugliest woman I've ever seen."

Mrs. Platz rolled her eyes in disgust. "That wasn't Tess, you dimwit. It was an old man!"

Stephanie and Ivan exchanged grimaces.

"Just exactly what happened?" Ivan asked.

Eileen Platz took a deep breath. "We were in bed. I was reading, and Frank was doing his crossword puzzle. And I started hearing creaking sounds, and then this rhythmic thumping and moaning . . ."

Ivan bit his lip and stared at his bare toes.

"I told Frank it was Tess, but he said it was

181

the wind, just like last night. So, I said he should get up and look, but would he do that? Nooooo."

"It didn't sound like a ghost to me," Mr. Platz said.

"Well, after a while it stopped, and I just lay there, waiting. Then it started again! And Frank *still* wouldn't go look out the window."

Stephanie felt the blush burning her ears. She cleared her throat and belted her robe a little tighter.

"After the moaning stopped this last time, there was a definite knocking at the windowpane. And a voice called 'Eileeeeen, Eileeeeen.' I think it was Tess. I can't be sure, of course, because it didn't introduce itself, but it was calling me!"

Stephanie looked at Mr. Platz. "Did you hear it, too?"

"Yeah. I almost made a mess in my pajamas. I tell you, I'm never going back in that room."

"Chickenheart wouldn't get out of bed," Eileen Platz said, throwing a vicious look at her husband, "so I got up and opened the shade. And there it was! Right in front of the window, looking right in at us as bold as could be!"

"Actually, it wasn't looking at us, Eileen. Its eyes were closed."

"That's true," she agreed, "but it could see through its eyelids. I could tell."

Stephanie already knew the answer to the next question, but she asked anyway. "What did this ghost look like?"

"It was an old man!"

"Was he wearing a gray suit?"

"No," Mrs. Platz said. "He had a raincoat on. One of those poncho things with a hood. It was raining, you know."

"Like wow," Melody said, "you really are cosmic. You must have drawn a brand-new ghost into the house."

Melody was weird, but she wasn't stupid. And Stephanie knew a patronizing tone when she heard it. Mrs. Platz, on the other hand, had obviously been settling her nerves with a large quantity of sherry and was willing to believe anything.

"So what happened to Mr. Ghost?" Stephanie asked. "Did he say anything else? Did he kick in your window?"

"No. He just was out there with his nose pressed against the glass, then he vanished. I accidentally screamed, and he went whooosh, straight up in the air."

Stephanie gave Mr. Platz what she hoped was a reassuring smile. "I can understand your reluctance to go back in the master bedroom. We'll get you settled into a room on the other side of the house, and I'm sure you won't be bothered by any more ghosts." She directed Melody to put fresh linens on the bed in room five and asked Lucy to bring Mr. and Mrs. Platz some hot cocoa and cookies from the kitchen. She motioned to Ivan to step out into the hall. "Have you checked the widow's walk and the cupola?" she asked him.

"Yes, but I'm going to check it again. We're obviously missing something," he said grimly. "This guy can't just disappear into thin air." He slid his feet into a pair of docksiders he'd retrieved from Stephanie's room. "Oh yeah, and while I'm busy checking out the house, why don't you try moving the bed away from the wall."

Stephanie shuffled into the kitchen and poured herself a cup of coffee from the pot heating on the stove. It had stopped raining, and the world looked fresh-scrubbed and shiny bright. It was going to be a glorious blue-sky day. She took a seat at the small kitchen table and helped herself to one of the bran muffins cooling on a wire rack.

Lucy pushed aside a small mound of fresh-chopped green pepper on the cutting board and turned to look at Stephanie. "Am I wrong, or did I see Ivan Rasmussen sauntering half-dressed from your room last night?"

Stephanie bit into the hot muffin and chewed. "We've become . . . friends."

Lucy brought her cousin a tub of butter and a knife and took a chair across from her. "Friends? Stephanie Elizabeth Lowe, I can tell from that goofy look on your face that you guys are a lot more than friends. I thought you were saving yourself for marriage? What about your virginity?"

"Gone," Stephanie said smugly.

Lucy groaned. "Stephanie, Stephanie, Stephanie. I warned you about him. He's a confirmed bachelor."

"I'm not so sure about that. I think he's just not ready for marriage." She buttered her muffin. "I'm not ready for marriage either."

"Why not?"

Stephanie laughed. "I don't know. Lots of reasons. I was seventeen for ten years. I have some growing up to do."

"Looks to me as if you're catching up fast."

Melody swung through the kitchen door and stood at the table, studying the muffins.

"You can eat one," Lucy said. "They're certified pig-free."

Melody took a muffin and sniffed it. "Hmmm." She nibbled a small piece. "So," she said to Stephanie, "are you sleeping with Rasmussen, or what?"

Lucy rolled her eyes. "Jeez, Melody, why don't you try being blunt?"

They stopped talking when Ivan pushed the kitchen door open. They looked at him for a second, then all three women blushed and turned their undivided attention to the muffins.

Ivan stood in the middle of the room with his hands in his jeans pockets. "Am I interrupting something?"

Melody pushed a strawlike strand of orange hair away from her face. "Lucy and I were just wondering if you and Stephanie are sleeping together now."

Ivan went to the stove and filled a mug with hot coffee. If anyone else had asked that question, he would have explained about tact and privacy, but Melody was hopeless, so he sipped his coffee, looked at Stephanie, and grinned. "The ball's in your court. You want to serve?"

"Not me," Stephanie said. "I wouldn't touch it."

Later that afternoon Ivan came up from the harbor and stopped short at the sidewalk in front of Haben. A large woman wrapped in a red-and-blue shawl was sitting on a folding chair on the widow's walk. She waved at him and smiled, and Ivan forced himself to smile back.

Stephanie met him at the door. "Did you see Mrs. Kowalsky?" Yes, by the look on his face, she could tell he had. "It turns out Mrs. Platz made national news, and we're swamped with room reservations. Ghost groupies. I moved Lucy in with Melody on the third floor."

She discovered that her palms were damp, and she silently cursed herself. She'd had sweaty palms too many times in her life. This time her life wasn't on the line—only her dignity. She wasn't sure which was worse.

"And I'd like to move you in with me. If that's okay with you. I'd adjust your rent," she added, faltering under his scrutiny.

He looked around and hated what he saw. Wall-to-wall people hoping to find a ghost, waiting for their turn on the widow's walk. Poor Tess.

Stephanie sighed. "I don't like it either," she admitted. "But I need the money."

"You need money this bad?"

"Ivan, I've invested every cent I own in this house. This is my sole source of income. Next September when you move your furniture out, I'll need to be able to buy furniture of my own."

"Why didn't you think of that before you bought the house?"

"I did. I had money set aside for a down payment on furniture, and I had to sink it into repairs on this relic."

Ivan didn't give a damn about the furniture or her mismanaging, but he was infuriated that she'd assume he'd be long gone by September.

"Move me anywhere you want," he said, keeping his voice tightly controlled.

He strode into the kitchen and took a cold beer from the refrigerator. He didn't want to say something in anger that he'd regret later. She was looking out for herself, and he couldn't blame her for that, but didn't she know how he felt about her? How could she possibly think he'd be gone in September?

Lucy stopped stirring a pot of chowder, fished in the junk drawer for a bottle opener, and handed it to Ivan. "That's imported lager. You need an opener. Although at second glance, you look mad enough to open that with your teeth."

He tipped the bottle back and took a long swallow. "Your cousin is driving me nuts."

Lucy made a sympathetic murmur, but she felt the laughter bubbling inside her. She'd always suspected when he finally fell in love it was going to be a real headfirst crash. Ivan didn't do things halfway. "Want to talk about it?"

"There's nothing to talk about. I sold Haben. She bought it, and she's turned it into a loony bin."

Lucy sighed. "Yeah. This hasn't worked out exactly as I'd expected. I think this ghost stuff has gotten out of hand."

"I think my feelings for Stephanie have gotten out of hand." He finished off his beer and looked in the chowder pot. "Smells good." A smile creased his face. "The first day out Stephanie made the *worst* chowder."

"I heard. She said you were great."

"She said that?"

"Um-hmm. She said you even ate some of it."

Ivan laughed. "I was hungry. *Really* hungry." Mostly hungry for Stephanie, he remembered. There was something about her, right from the start, that was so damn attractive. He liked the way she'd rolled down the hill and landed on her back with a good healthy expletive on her lips. She wasn't fragile. For some inexplicable reason that made him feel all the more protective of her.

The sound of loud laughter and breaking glass carried into the kitchen. "I'm hating this more all the time," Lucy said.

Melody stomped in with a dustpan filled with glass shards. "These people have to go. They are *boring*."

"I think we have to look at priorities here," Lucy said to Melody. "Know what I mean?"

"Yeah," Melody said, "we have to get rid of these disgusting people. And then we have to get Ivan and Stephanie out of that little room. The bed squeaks. You can hear it all through the house. I hardly slept a wink last night."

Ivan got another beer. He wasn't a prude, but he wasn't an exhibitionist either. Going public with his sex life wasn't high on his list of anticipated accomplishments. He felt himself blushing for the first time in his life and rested the cold bottle on his forehead.

Stephanie pushed through the kitchen door, went straight to the sink, and soaked a dish towel. She plopped the towel over her head, not caring that the water was running off and dripping onto the floor.

"I'm getting a migraine. I've never had a migraine in my life, but I'm getting one now." She whipped the towel away and stood up straighter. "There. That feels better," she said, turning to Lucy.

"All these people want dinner. That means we have to have two seatings. Ivan can preside over the first seating while Melody and I serve. Then I'll take charge of the second seating while you and Melody serve." Stephanie looked at everyone in the kitchen. "How does that sound?"

Lucy raised an eyebrow. "You think these people need a master of ceremonies?"

"No. I think they need keepers. Animal trainers. You think Sears sells cattle prods?"

Stephanie leaned against the counter. There has to be a better way of getting furniture money, she thought. Controlling this crowd of

ghost chasers made police work seem tame.
And Ivan was mad at her. She couldn't blame
him. She'd stripped Haben of its dignity.

She took a basket of toasted bread rounds
and slid them into the microwave for ten seconds. When the house quieted down later,
she'd have a chance to think. Right now all she
wanted to do was get everyone fed as effi-
ciently as possible. She removed the bread and
grabbed a crock of butter from the refrigerator.
"Melody, everyone starts out with a cup of
chowder."

Melody took the can of spray starch from the
pantry shelf and freshened up her hair. Then
she gave Lucy a thumbs-up and took a tray of
chowder cups out to the dining room.

"You want some chowder?" she asked the
man on Ivan's left. Without waiting for a
reply, she slammed a cup down in front of
him. "Watch out for the fish eyes. I read
someplace that fish eyes are poisonous. They
make your tongue swell up so big it doesn't
fit in your mouth, and it turns black, then you
choke to death. You ever see anyone choke to
death?"

The man shook his head.

"It's not pretty," Melody said. "It's slow. Real

slow. Your eyes bug out of your head, your face gets purple, and your testicles swell up as big as watermelons, and when you finally die, you make a mess in your pants."

"I read that article," a woman at the other end of the table said. "It was in the May issue of *Reader's Digest*, wasn't it?"

The woman next to her shook her head. "I read *Reader's Digest* from cover to cover, and I know for a fact that there was no such article. It was in one of those health magazines they have in doctors' offices. I remember seeing it while I was waiting to get my blood pressure checked. I remember because the man in the photograph didn't have any eyes. They'd fallen clear out of his head."

Melody looked at Ivan and whispered from the side of her mouth, "If there's one thing I can't stand, it's being upstaged."

She distributed two more cups of chowder and stopped beside a fat man with a florid face. "Sometimes the poison liquid leaks out of the eyeballs and contaminates the whole pot of chowder," she said. "But that only happens when you overcook the eyeballs, and we were careful not to do that."

She looked at Stephanie, who was standing

frozen with a basket of bread in her hand. "Lucy didn't overcook the chowder again, did she?"

Stephanie only stared at her in astonishment. During the past couple of weeks she'd thought of Melody as a rebellious teenager, but she suddenly had a flash of insight, seeing her as an entirely different person. She suspected Melody wasn't flaky at all. And she had serious doubts about her being a teenager. Melody was a performer; Stephanie was sure of it. And she had a wicked sense of humor.

Stephanie bit back a smile and wondered how she could have missed something that was now so obvious. She felt as if she were looking in that rearview mirror again, seeing an outlandish parody of herself as a cop being a teenager. She couldn't even begin to guess what Melody was up to. Instinct told her it wasn't anything bad. Self-preservation kept her from believing it one hundred percent.

"I'm sure the chowder's fine," Stephanie said. She leaned over Ivan's shoulder, and whispered in his ear, "Better not eat it, just in case. I'd hate to see you try to fit a pair of watermelons in those tight jeans."

"I understand you're the young lady who

talks to Tess," one of the women said to Melody.

"Yup."

"What sort of things does she say to you?"

Melody shrugged. "We talk about Eminem a lot. She's heavy into Eminem."

The woman looked confused. "You talk about M & Ms?"

"No. The rapper Eminem. Jeez." Melody began collecting soup cups. "Mr. Jackson, you didn't eat a drop of your chowder. How are you going to grow up big and strong that way? Oh, Mr. Billings, you didn't eat yours either."

"I'm saving myself for the main course," Mr. Billings said. "What are we having tonight?"

Melody's mouth curved ever so slightly. "Ham."

Chapter 9

Stephanie left the cranberry glass hurricane lamp burning in the downstairs hall and crept up the stairs. She'd shut the widow's walk down at ten and advised everyone to go to bed and wait for ghosts. Then she'd said a silent apology to Tess and warned her to stay away from the master bedroom. Mr. and Mrs. Billings were in the master bedroom, and they were enough to frighten the ectoplasm out of anyone, dead or alive. She went to her room and quickly changed into jeans, a black turtleneck, and a heavy black sweatshirt. Then she quietly went downstairs and out the back door.

She took a deep breath, letting the sharp night air fill her lungs while her eyes adjusted to the darkness. She waved acknowledgment when Ivan signaled from behind the concealing lower branches of a giant spruce. He'd chosen good cover, she thought, moving to join him. She wouldn't have seen him if he hadn't flashed the light at her. She drew closer, and the jaded cop part of her went momentarily speechless at the picniclike atmosphere Ivan had created. He'd spread a blanket on twenty years' accumulation of pine needles and brought a second blanket, a searchlight, binoculars, and a thermos of coffee. "Looks as if you're planning on spending the night," she said.

"This is my first stakeout. I wanted to be prepared." And he wanted to make her comfortable. He wanted to keep her warm and safe and entertained. He would have rented a Winnebago if he thought he could have gotten away with it. Or better yet, he would have hired a detective and let him sit out here, freezing his buns, while Stephanie was inside, soaking in a hot bubble bath. And after the bubble bath . . .

Stephanie shifted uncomfortably. She'd never had a stakeout partner look at her quite the way Ivan was looking at her. It wasn't difficult to guess what was on his mind, and it was almost impossible not to respond. She knew if she gave him the slightest encouragement, they'd be in the house, under the covers, and the mystery would remain unsolved.

Maybe it would be worth it. It wasn't much of a mystery, anyway. It wasn't as if there were drugs involved. And in actuality, no one had gotten hurt. There was just a dead guy who turned up every now and then, and he'd been dead a long time. He could hang around a little longer while they took a night off to make love.

She took a moment to think about it seriously and decided there weren't many things more important than making love to Ivan. She finally understood the enormous importance of the bedroom. It was a place where love was exchanged and strengthened, and the more time she spent with Ivan, the less she understood promiscuity and infidelity. There was a bond growing between them. A collection of shared intimacies, adventures, problems, and dreams. Private whisperings held them together as surely as steel bands, and she couldn't imagine ever wanting to sever those ties.

Priorities, she thought. It was important to get her priorities straight. Ivan and Haben were at the top of the list, but it was a toss-up for the number one slot. Her emotional choice was definitely Ivan, but her more practical intellect insisted on Haben. She owned Haben. She was responsible for it, and it would guarantee her security in her old age. Someone was threatening her success as an innkeeper, and she had to find out who and why.

Ivan had watched the transformation take place inside her by studying her face. For a minute there, he'd almost had her. Then a variety of emotions had tramped across, ending in steely-eyed resignation, and he knew they'd be playing cop for a while longer. "Determined to get to the root of it?"

Stephanie looked grim, not completely happy with her choice. "Yeah. I hope this works. I'd dearly love to know who broke my toilet."

Ivan pulled her onto the blanket. "I think you have a toilet fixation. You're almost as bad as Melody and pork chops. Besides, how do you know the flying dead man has anything to do with your bathroom?"

"Woman's intuition." Stephanie sprawled on her stomach and felt Ivan move next to her, cuddling into her side, throwing his leg over hers. "Ivan Rasmussen, what do you think you're doing?"

"Sharing body heat."

"As long as you don't share too much. I wouldn't want to be so distracted that I missed the corpse dangler."

"Spoilsport." His hand inched under her sweatshirt. Stephanie murmured an unintelligible warning, and Ivan responded with a gentle squeeze. "Just warming my hand."

Yeah, right. Stephanie didn't think his hand felt cold at all. It felt nice and warm. And it was performing skillful manipulations that were encouraging more of the doodah humming.

"You know what you need? You need some hot coffee. Hot coffee will warm you up," she said, pushing at Ivan, trying to wriggle out from under him.

"Maybe later. I'm warming up just fine now."

"Yes, but will you be able to sprint across that yard if you have to?"

Ivan sighed. "I bet you were a terrific cop. Certainly never corrupted by forbidden temptations."

"I had my moments." She sat cross-legged and tugged her sweatshirt into place, turning her attention to the house. "What do you think of Melody?"

"I think she's a fraud."

"You have any idea who she is?"

"Not a clue, but she has a lot of nerve and a sinful sense of humor." Ivan opened the thermos, and the rich aroma of strong coffee rushed out in a swirl of steam. "I didn't pick up on her until tonight at the dinner table. I saw the expression on your face and knew you'd caught on, too."

"I've been thinking about it. The reason we finally caught on is that she shifted her position. Up until tonight, we were the ones being tricked. Tonight she changed sides and threw in with us—at least for a while."

"You sound cynical."

Stephanie took a sip of coffee and returned the cup to Ivan. "She lied to us. You should be cynical, too."

"You lied to a lot of people when you went undercover. Sometimes there are good reasons."

She knew he was right, and she liked Melody, but she knew the danger of being betrayed by someone close. You kept your eyes open for the bad guys, but if you misjudged a friend, you were left hideously vulnerable. In undercover work it could cost you your life. She'd learned that the hard way. She reminded herself that this wasn't undercover work and was most likely some goofy prank, but that was an intellectual conclusion and had little effect on the apprehension she felt.

They sat on the blanket in companionable silence for a long time. Finally, Ivan looked at his watch and sighed. "For two nights now, some idiot has dangled a dead body in front of the rear windows. Where is he tonight? Why is it you can never find a sicko when you want one?"

Stephanie kept her eyes on the house. "Now you know the truth about police work. Hours of tedium, occasionally livened up by a few moments of sheer terror."

A chill ran along Ivan's spine. He didn't know what sort of terrors she'd experienced in the past, but he was going to make sure her future was free from that sort of fear. He wrapped her in the extra blanket and drew her into the circle of his arms so they were sitting her back to his front. "I'm glad I didn't know you when you were undercover. I wouldn't have been able to deal with the terror."

"Undercover was cushy. I was always scared

to death they might reassign me to traffic detail. I knew a school crossing guard who got her toes run over by a Volkswagen."

He understood what she was saying, just as he understood that statistically air travel was safer than driving in a car, but those statistics didn't make planes or police work any more appealing to him. He touched her hair with the tips of his fingers and wondered how she got it so silky. He felt the heat return and searched for a diversion. "Tell me more about being a cop. Did you like it?"

"Yup. It was the right thing for me to do at that point in my life. It wasn't dramatic like on television. It was a job, and it gave me a sense of purpose. I think I basically have a blue-collar mentality. I like jobs that are physical. I wouldn't be good sitting behind a desk all day making decisions or analyzing computer printouts."

"I bet you were a good cop."

"I was okay. Until the end."

More silence stretched between them while Stephanie ran through the end in her mind, just as she always did when she thought of her life in Jersey City. She could feel Ivan watching her, feel the invisible support his presence always brought, and she knew he wanted to know more. She was surprised to find that she wanted to tell him more. He was a good partner. A good listener. A good friend.

He stretched his legs and leaned back on one elbow. "Are you going to tell me about it?"

"About being a cop?" She was hedging, she thought. Old habits die hard.

"About the end. Why did you quit?"

"Going for the jugular, huh?" Stephanie asked.

"I've been patient."

She nodded. It was true. He'd been patient. And besides, the wound had healed. The embarrassment and disillusionment of her past had faded beside the glorious vitality of love and lust. "Okay. You want the long story or the short story?"

"The long story."

Stephanie poured out the last cup of coffee and sipped slowly.

"When I graduated from the Police Academy, I didn't look a day over sixteen, so I was the perfect person to plant in the schools. It was very small-time crime. All they wanted was to find out who the abusers were so they could get them into rehab and get rid of the pushers in the hallways and playgrounds. As I got older I gradually did more counseling and PR than undercover work.

"Then last fall two college kids I knew got hold of some bad stuff and died. They were good kids. Played basketball and thought they needed an edge, I guess. Turned out there was a lot of this junk floating around on the local campus. They needed someone with experience to find out where the stuff was coming from, and I was assigned to the project."

She made a disgusted sound. "It was stupid of me to accept the assignment. I let my emotions and my ego override my good sense. I didn't fit into the college scene, and I didn't have the professional maturity to play with the big boys.

"Anyway, I graduated from high school to college and went undercover for four months. I was working with a federal agent named Amos Anderson, and one day he set up a meeting with a dealer at one of the Prentice Avenue piers. It was February, and the wind was blowing so bad across the pier the seagulls were flying backward. We stood there waiting, and after a while a big black limo pulled up and four people got out. Three kneebreakers and a suit, and as soon as I saw them I started to sweat. We were out there on this godforsaken pier with no place to go, and my knees were knocking together so bad you could hear them in Hoboken.

"The man in the suit walked right up to us, holding his hat on his head with both hands. 'Windy,' he shouted to us. 'Yeah,' we answered. 'Lonely out here on a Sunday.' "

Stephanie gave her head a disbelieving shake. "No kidding. Who else but two crazy cops would be standing on a deserted pier in gale-force winds with a chill factor of twenty below?

"So the guy looked at Amos and said, 'I understand you want to buy.' Amos was such a pro. He came from Miami, and he'd been through this a hundred times. He just shrugged and said, maybe. They started talking, and in the middle of the transaction, the man turned to me, looked me in the eye, and said, 'You're a cop, aren't you?' It was the first time I'd ever known absolute, total terror. I heard an overcoat rustle open, and the guy behind me put a gun to my head . . . right here."

She pointed to a spot just to the side of her temple and realized her hand was shaking and thought it would probably shake for the rest of her life, every time she told this story. "I swear, my heart was pounding so loud it drowned out all other sounds. I was so scared, I was dizzy, and the next thing I knew, I was flying through the air and sinking like a stone in the river. I came up next to the cement pilings, and by the time I got myself to shore, there must have been forty agents on the pier.

"Thank heaven Amos had been smart enough to pre-position backups. When everything started going wrong, he managed to knock the gun away from my head. People tell me he picked me up and threw me into the river like a Frisbee. I'd be dead if he hadn't."

"How'd they find out you were a cop?"

"One of the other women working undercover was setting up her own retirement plan, compliments of the mob. She'd provided them with photographs of all the narcs and all the undercover people, and this guy suddenly recognized me."

She was amazed at how easy it had been to retell the story. A few weeks ago she could hardly bear to think about it. She'd crammed a lot of personal growth into a few weeks. Because of Ivan, she thought. It seemed as if she'd known him all her life. He'd given her other things to think about besides death and stupidity.

"I stayed with the case until we wrapped it up, but I'd changed. Somewhere between the pier and the river, my love affair with law enforcement died a quick death. I asked myself, did I want to spend the rest of my life getting tossed into the Hudson River? And the answer was no.

"Looking back, I think I was just burned out. I was tired of being submerged in an adolescent world. I was becoming jaded by the easy access and the acceptance of drugs. It was starting to seem too normal to me. When I was standing on that pier with a gun at my head, I should have been outraged, but I wasn't. I was just plain scared. Somewhere along the line I'd stopped being a tough idealist."

Ivan took the empty cup from her and screwed it back onto the thermos. "I don't think so. If you'd really stopped being a tough idealist, you wouldn't care that you'd stopped. You just needed a vacation. Maybe your views on life were adjusting to meet more realistic expectations. That happens as we get older," he said, smiling.

"Did that happen to you?"

"To some extent. I have a better sense of my limitations. That doesn't mean I always live within them," he added ruefully.

Stephanie caught a flash of movement at the top of the house and put a silencing hand on Ivan's arm. "The cupola," she whispered. Someone was up there, moving onto the widow's walk. No moon. No stars. Nature wasn't helping out, Stephanie thought, straining to see. A second form appeared. It stood ramrod straight, and Stephanie shivered. "Tell me that's not a body bag."

Ivan only grunted. It was obviously a body bag, and it was filled with a body. A big, stiff, dead body.

The black plastic body bag was lowered by rope down the sloping roof and dangled at the second-story level for a minute before being cut loose. It hit the ground with a sickening thud that made Stephanie and Ivan recoil in horror. They waited a moment while the person on the widow's walk retreated, then they ran to the inert form lying on the ground. Ivan partially unzipped the bag.

"It's the old guy in the gray suit." He zipped the bag back up and pulled Stephanie across the lawn, back to the spruce tree, where they flopped on the ground, panting.

Stephanie gasped for air. "Do you think anyone saw us?"

"Only the guy in the body bag, and he looked as though he could keep a secret."

The back door opened and a dark figure emerged. It went directly to the bag, covered it with leaves, and scuttled back into the house.

"That's why I could never find him," Ivan said. "They've been pitching him out windows and off roofs and covering him with leaves. I never thought to look under that huge pile of leaves."

"This is disgusting. What kind of a person are we dealing with? Someone who throws bodies off roofs?"

There was the sound of a car pulling into the driveway. Headlights briefly flashed on the carriage house that had been converted into a garage, then were extinguished. A battered pickup truck crept along in the dark and stopped. Stephanie caught her breath when Melody got out of the pickup, lowered the tailgate, took a carton from the back of the truck, and carefully carried it into the house.

"This is really strange," Stephanie said. "I

haven't any idea what's going on. I can't even begin to guess."

"You think we should go in and find out?"

She shook her head. "Let's stay here a while longer. See what happens next."

Half an hour later, lights flashed on in all the upstairs rooms. Doors slammed, windows were thrown open. Lights appeared in the downstairs rooms, and people began pouring out. Stephanie and Ivan left their cover to investigate.

Mr. Billings reeled off the front porch. "Man, what a stench. I've been at lots of ghost sightings, but I've *never* smelled anything like this."

"It's a ghost from hell," Melody said.

Mr. Billings buttoned his overcoat over his pajamas. "*Nothing* could get me to go back in there."

"But Mr. Billings," Melody said, "your clothes are in there. You're paid up for the night."

"I don't care if I'm paid up for the year. Here's my address. Send my clothes UPS."

Two cars pulled out of the side yard parking area and disappeared down the street.

Melody smiled at the departing cars. "Gee, what a shame, everyone's leaving."

The heavyset woman in the shawl stood on the sidewalk and looked at the house. "This happen often?"

"Yeah," Melody said. "Sometimes it smells like this all winter. You get used to it."

The woman sniffed her shawl. "It's in my clothes."

"If you let them air out for a couple weeks, they should be okay," Melody told her. "It's the slime stains that don't come out. You were lucky you weren't slimed. Well, I think the worst of it's over. We can all go back to sleep now."

The woman pressed her lips together. "Are you crazy? I'm not going back in there."

Melody put her arm around the woman. "Don't worry about the slime. It almost always comes *before* the smell."

"I don't think this house is haunted. I think it's possessed. And I think you're one step away from the funny farm."

Melody narrowed her eyes. "No need to get personal about this."

The woman picked up her suitcase and turned on her heel. "I'm leaving. And I'm not paying for my room."

"Fine," Melody said. "You don't like rude

ghosts? That's okay by me. I understand. Sorry this didn't work out for you."

Lucy was on the front lawn, fanning the air around her. "Ghost from hell?"

"I couldn't stand those people a second longer," Melody said. "They were so boring."

Stephanie kept her distance from the house. "According to my calculations, we haven't a single guest left."

"With friends like Melody, you don't need enemies," Ivan whispered.

"So, you think Melody's responsible for this?"

"Yup. Don't you?"

"I think she's responsible for the smell. I can't believe she's responsible for the dead man and all the things that have been going wrong with my house." She tried not to smile. "I hate to admit it, and I'd never tell Melody, but I'm definitely relieved to be rid of those people. They were awful." She backed farther down the sidewalk. "What *is* that smell?"

"Grade A Maine stink bomb," Ivan said. "I used to make them all the time when I was a kid."

"I bet you were really popular."

"I could close a school down with one of those."

"Is it going to last long?"

"Somewhere between a day and a week. I'd say closer to a week. This one is pretty powerful. Whoever made this was a master stink bomb maker."

Lucy ambled over to them. "Smells like one of your stink bombs, Ivan."

"Yup."

"Clever," she said.

"I didn't do it."

Lucy looked surprised. "You're the only one I know who can build a stink bomb like that." She looked at Stephanie. "He was great. He used to close down the school!"

They heard the motor catch on the pickup at the rear of the house and turned in time to see the truck peel out of the driveway. Even in the dark, it was easy to recognize Melody's orange hair. A second person sat beside her.

Stephanie grabbed Ivan's arm. "It's Melody! And she's with someone."

"Yeah. Probably the body tosser."

Stephanie felt the disappointment squeezing her heart. She could forgive Melody for the stink bomb. Desecrating the dead was some-thing else. "They're getting away."

"And they've probably got the body," Ivan said, walking to the backyard, giving a wide berth to the house.

Lucy tagged along. "Somebody want to tell me what you're talking about?"

"We saw someone throw the old geezer in the gray suit off the roof. And then we saw Melody drive that pickup into the yard and take a box into the house." Ivan kicked at the scattered leaves. "This is where they hid the body. It's gone, of course."

Lucy yawned. "I'd probably be more excited about this if I hadn't spent the past fourteen hours cooking and cleaning up after ten people who would have tried the patience of Mother Teresa. I'm too tired to think about mysterious dead guys. It's after midnight, and I'm beat. I'm going to hold my breath and dash into the house to retrieve my purse, then I'm going to move in with my parents until Haben smells better."

Ivan took Stephanie's hand. "Let's open some windows and lock up the downstairs. We can spend the night on the *Savage*."

"I hate to go off and just leave Haben empty.

Suppose one of the guests decides to come back?"

"Believe me, no one is coming back to Haben tonight."

"Suppose Melody comes back?"

Ivan gathered her to him and pressed a kiss to her temple. "I don't think she will."

Stephanie fought back tears. "How could she do this to me? I trusted her."

"Let's let it rest for tonight and pick it up in the morning when we're not so tired," Ivan said.

"That poor dead man. My Lord, they've been throwing him out windows and dropping him off roofs."

He had to admit, it was pretty grisly.

Stephanie gave an involuntary shiver. "It's like a horror movie. *Invasion of the Punk Body Snatchers.* I was wrong not to call the police. I suppose all along I expected it to turn out to be some tasteless practical joke."

"Maybe that's all it is."

"You don't sound very convinced." She shook her head. "No. I've got to report this."

He didn't want her to. Not yet. First he had to do some investigating of his own. "Wait a while longer. At least until tomorrow." Ivan's eyes focused on her mouth. His lips softened and brushed against hers. "You know what we need? We need a fun activity. Like going to bed."

Half an hour later Ivan closed the hatch cover to the aft cabins and lit one of the two oil lamps that hung suspended from the small salon ceiling. He started a fire in the delft fireplace and stood in front of it for a moment, warming his hands, trying to dispel the feeling of unease that sat heavy in his stomach. Something very odd was happening, and he had a sick feeling that it involved old friends.

Tomorrow he was going to get to the root of it, but for the moment he was going to try to forget about it and concentrate on Stephanie. He finally had her alone—really alone—and he intended to make the most of it.

"You know, the best way to survive in the cold is to get naked with a friend."

Stephanie's breath came out in a cloud of frost as she huddled in a wool blanket. "That's a vicious rumor started a hundred years ago by some pervert who didn't have central heating."

She was looking forward to snuggling with Ivan in the cozy bunk, but she couldn't imagine taking her clothes off in the freezing cabin. She tapped her toes and wrapped the blanket tighter, waiting for the fire to bake away the chill and the dampness, hoping it would happen soon. "So you think this fire's going to get us toasty, huh?"

"You look doubtful."

"It's not a very big fireplace."

"It's not a very big room," he said, going into his cabin and returning with a bottle of brandy and two snifters. He poured the brandy and handed one of the glasses to Stephanie. "Here's to love and friendship and honesty."

Stephanie sipped the brandy and felt fire burn down her throat and race through her body. She took another sip, and the vertebrae in her back relaxed. "Were you thinking of Melody when you made that toast?"

He slid his hands inside her blanket, his fingers massaging lazy circles on either side of her spine. "No. I was thinking of us."

She was growing deliciously warm deep inside. It was a drugging liquid heat, working its way along her spine, moving like hot molasses to her toes and fingertips. She set her glass on the table and let the blanket slip from her shoulders.

"This looks promising," Ivan said. "Getting hot?"

"It's the brandy."

"Mmmm. I keep it for medical emergencies."

Stephanie moved closer, fitting herself into all the hollows and crevices that naturally occurred between men and women. "Am I a medical emergency?"

"No. But I would have been one if you hadn't warmed up."

He kissed her, and the kiss lingered while his hands roamed over her body, rekindling a passion that had never been completely extinguished. And no matter how much loving they did, he thought, this passion would always smolder. He would never have enough of her. Never tire of her. Never stop loving her. He eased her onto his bunk and quickly stripped her of her clothes. He knew all her secrets now. He knew exactly where to touch, where to kiss, where to tease.

"I could get used to this," Stephanie said. "Sunlight and fresh sea air spilling in through an open window, the lingering aroma of a wood fire from the night before, and a handsome man bringing me my morning coffee."

Ivan sat on the edge of his bunk and watched her. She was warm and rumpled-looking in his T-shirt, and she smelled wonderful—an exotic blend of pine needles, flowery shampoo, and sex. "Is that all I am to you? A handsome man?" His tone was teasing, but his question was serious.

"Maybe a little more."

He continued to watch.

"Maybe a lot more," she amended.

He wondered if it was the right time, decided it wasn't. And knew he was going to ask anyway. "Will you marry me?"

The question hung in the air while time seemed to stand still. She stared at him wide-eyed, never noticing that she'd slopped coffee over the rim of the mug onto her hand.

Ivan grabbed a towel and mopped up. "Took you by surprise, huh?"

"Are you serious?"

He recognized the panic on her face and silently cursed himself for being so blunt. He should have waited and taken her out to a nice restaurant, brought her flowers. He wasn't good at this. He'd spent his whole life avoiding ties and entanglements. He'd asked her to marry him in the same tone of voice he would have used to offer her hockey tickets.

He kissed the hand she'd spilled coffee on and tried it again. "I love you, Steph, and I want to marry you." You can't get much more serious than this, he thought. It wasn't a frivolous, spur-of-the-moment decision. He'd waited for her for a long time, and he knew it was right.

Stephanie couldn't remember ever feeling so totally flustered. Marriage! She still hadn't completely gotten used to the idea of having a lover. "It's so sudden," she stammered. "I wasn't expecting this." In her heart she might have been *wanting* it, but she definitely hadn't been *expecting* it.

"I can give you some time, if that's what you need. We have all winter to get to know each other."

It wasn't a matter of time, she thought. It was a matter of . . . she didn't know.

"Do you love me?"

"Yes." And she realized she felt secure in that love. What she felt for Ivan wasn't infatuation. It was real. She couldn't imagine ever loving anyone more.

"Then think about it."

She nodded. "I'll think about it as soon as I stop hyperventilating."

He took the coffee cup from her and kicked the cabin door closed. "I know a good remedy for hyperventilation."

Chapter 10

The noxious odor still clung to the curtains and upholstery, but with the windows wide open and a table fan blowing full tilt, the upstairs bathroom was usable. Stephanie dashed from the shower, jumped into clothes purchased half an hour before, and ran from the house. Ivan snagged her on the front lawn and wrapped a dry towel around her wet hair. "Did you see the ghost from hell while you were in there?" he asked jokingly.

Stephanie patted her towel-wrapped head, and said, "The ghost from hell is probably in Kansas City right now with Melody."

"I don't think so."

She raised her eyebrows.

"I recognized the truck she was driving, and it wasn't from Kansas City."

"Are you kidding me? Why didn't you tell me last night?"

Ivan buttoned her into a new wool jacket. "We were busy last night."

She felt a flush of heat at the memory. "Mmmm, so we were."

"Since the inn is indefinitely closed, and we have some time on our hands, I think we should go for a drive in the country and look up Melody."

Forty-five minutes later they left Route 1 for a secondary road. Stephanie studied the smooth leather upholstery of Ivan's black SUV, thinking the car suited him—but then so would a Viper. He was a complicated person. Full of surprises and contradictions.

He'd been silent since they'd left Camden, and she knew he was giving her time to reorganize her thoughts about their relationship. About marriage. *Marriage.* Lord, she could hardly run the word through her mind without feeling hysteria bubble up in her throat. Ivan Rasmussen wanted to marry her. It was beyond her wildest dreams. It was flattering. It was frightening. It was hard to believe. Stephanie Rasmussen. Preposterous. And wonderful.

They passed a small town, nothing more than a gas station, an all-purpose store, and a small white church. A few unimaginative ranch-style houses had been built close to the road, a two-story farmhouse sat farther back, surrounded by bleak fields. The term *hardscrabble farm* came to mind. She wondered if the owner of the truck lived on one of these no-frills farms.

"You've been very quiet," she said. "You haven't told me who owns the truck Melody was driving."

"Ted Grisham, the man who taught me how to make stink bombs."

Stephanie rubbed her hands together. "The plot thickens. Who's Ted Grisham?"

"A friend," he said tersely.

"Ouch."

"Yeah. That's what I think, too." Ivan slowed as they approached another little town of neat yards and small, well-tended houses. At the northern edge of town he pulled into the parking lot of a large brick structure that reminded her of the Knox Woolen Mill in Camden. "What is this?"

Ivan sighed and slumped in his seat. "This is"—he took a deep breath—"Rasmussen

Leather Products. When I inherited Haben, I also inherited this." He pinched the bridge of his nose with his thumb and forefinger. "It's a shoe factory."

"You don't look too happy about it."

"I hate it. I've hated it all my life. I don't even like to *wear* shoes."

Stephanie grinned because the image of Ivan Rasmussen as a shoe baron was ludicrous, and because while he was trying to sound disgusted, it was obvious from the way his voice cracked that he saw the humor in it, too.

"It's not funny," he said, smiling. "Well, yeah, I guess it is sort of funny. Can you imagine me running a shoe factory?"

"No."

"My great-great-grandfather started this leather business when there was an abundance of hides in the area. Over the years it evolved into a shoe factory. Unfortunately, as you saw during the ride here, this shoe factory is the only industry for miles. People in this town have lived and worked here for generations. Without Rasmussen Leather Products the town would die."

He got out of the car and opened the passenger door for Stephanie. "We'll walk to Ted's house. It's just down the street. Ted is the factory foreman. When I was a kid my dad used to bring me here to see the shoes. I hated the factory, but I loved Ted. He knew how to skip stones across the river behind the factory, and he could spit farther than anyone on the face of the earth . . ."

"And he knew how to make stink bombs."

"Yup. He knew how to make stink bombs."

He picked a stone up and sailed it through the air, into the back end of the parking lot. "When my dad died, I took a look at the books of this sad old factory and discovered it had been running in the red. I loved my dad. He was a good man, and he wasn't stupid, but he had no talent for running a business. No one had made any improvements in this place in fifty years. It was in such bad shape, I couldn't get anyone to loan me money to modernize it."

Stephanie stopped walking and looked at him. "My Lord, you sold Haben to save this factory, didn't you?"

"All these people would have been out of jobs. I couldn't do that to them." He threw his arm around her and started her walking again.

"Anyway, once I made some initial changes,

I was able to persuade a bank to finance the rest. And I changed the direction of the product. Went back to making quality, hand-sewn shoes. Just a few styles. Docksiders and classic Wellingtons. It'll take a while before it's on its feet, but I think if the operation stays simple, it can eventually turn a nice profit. Hopefully I can get my nose out of it soon and let the factory go back to running itself."

Stephanie felt a lump-in-the-throat surge of love and respect for the man next to her. She was proud of him. Proud to be his lover and his friend. And his wife? How about his wife? She shivered and took a deep breath. Stephanie Rasmussen. *Yikes!*

Ivan stopped in front of a freshly painted white house that looked like all the other white houses, and he pointed to a maroon pickup in the driveway. "Look familiar?"

The kitchen door to the little Cape Cod slammed shut. A dog barked, raced into the driveway, stopped short, and ran back into the yard. The sound of voices carried over the noise of the excited dog. Stephanie and Ivan exchanged glances.

"I know that voice," Stephanie said.

"I think we hit the jackpot."

No one noticed them when they walked

around to the back, because everyone was too absorbed in the problem at hand. Melody and Lucy each had a handle on the black plastic body bag stuck half-in and half-out of the small basement window.

"This is impossible," Lucy said. "We should have taken him up the stairs the way I wanted."

Melody dug her heels in and pulled. "It seemed like a shortcut. I mean, we always dumped him out of windows before."

"Yes, but they were *big* windows," Ivan said.

Both women yelped and dropped the bag. The body slid back through the window and landed with a muffled thunk. A third familiar voice could be heard cursing in the basement.

Ivan raised his eyebrows. "Ace?"

"I've sort of adopted him," Melody said. "Daddy's giving him a job at the factory."

Things began to come together in Ivan's mind. "My Lord, you're Ted's daughter. The skinny kid who went to Juilliard."

"And when I graduated from Juilliard, I went on tour with a band, but I found out I wasn't the touring type, so I came home. Thanks to you, I have a home to come home to."

Ivan turned his attention to Lucy. "What are you doing here?"

"Helping cousin Melody. We have to return Mr. Kulecza."

"I didn't know Melody was a cousin," Stephanie said.

Lucy nodded. "On my mother's side. I guess that makes you cousins-in-law or something."

There were a lot of scuffing and thumping noises coming from the house. The door was flung open, and Ace backed out, dragging the bag. He saw Ivan and paled. "Oh crap!"

Ivan pointed at the bag. "Mr. Kulecza?"

"It's not really as bad as it seems," Melody said. "I can explain."

Ivan had a flashback of past conversations about broken pigs' legs and cancerous growths and wasn't sure he wanted to hear the explanation.

Melody saw the tense set to his mouth and decided not to wait for encouragement.

"Everyone in town was really upset when they found out you had to put Haben up for sale to save the factory. We tried to raise enough money to pay for the changes ourselves, but we couldn't even come close. Then Lucy had a brainstorm. She found out Stephanie had just come into a ton of money and wanted to leave New Jersey. It was too good to be true. Not only would Stephanie be the perfect person to buy Haben, but she'd be the perfect person to match up with you. All we had to do was get you two to fall in love and get married, and you could live Habenly ever after."

Ivan stood statue still while he absorbed what he'd just heard. The whole damn town had plotted to get him married. And worse than that, they'd plotted to get him back into Haben. He felt like a gold digger! An opportunist! He was touched by their concern, and he was furious at their meddling.

"Just exactly what did you do to ensure we'd fall in love?"

Melody backed up a step at the controlled anger in his voice. "Well, we thought it would be good if we could get Stephanie to take a cruise, but she wouldn't cooperate. Lucy tried all summer to get her on the boat, but no, Stephanie didn't have time. So as a last resort we came up with this plan to get her on board as cook. We broke a whole lot of stuff and set her up with workmen who would overcharge, then when we knew her money was short, we offered her Stanley Shelton."

Stephanie gasped. "You wasted my money! How could you do that? I needed that money."

"We couldn't think of anything else to do. Besides, we have almost all of it in a bank account for you. Lenny Schneider fixed your porch for free, and Hyram Mayler didn't actually give you a new water heater . . . he gave you your old water heater back. The only thing we didn't count on was the toilet. It got cracked by accident. I haven't any idea how your toilet got cracked."

A muscle twitched in Ivan's jaw. "Why did you stow away on the *Savage?*"

"To keep an eye on you." Melody defiantly stuck her nose into the air in response to his threatening tone. "We weren't sure how much pirate blood you'd inherited."

"I see." He looked at Stephanie, who was standing rigid at his side. Her face was set in a mask of grim disbelief. He curled his hand around her waist, nestling her a little closer, and gestured at the body bag. "Mr. Kulecza. Doesn't he have any relatives? I can't believe someone gave you this guy to throw out of windows."

Laughter flashed across Melody's face. "He's just a dummy. We borrowed him from Zembrowsky's Funeral Home. My cousin Joey works there. They use Mr. Kulecza to show off the caskets. They named him Mr. Kulecza because he looks like Bucky Kulecza. Remember old Bucky? Used to make lasts?" Melody stooped to unzip the bag. "He's really lifelike. They use this same stuff to make the robots at Disneyland.

"Things didn't look as if they were going so well between you guys, so we thought we'd borrow Mr. Kulecza, dangle him in front of Stephanie's window in the middle of the night, and she'd get scared and turn to you. It sounded great when we thought of it, but dopey Ace stashed Mr. Kulecza in the wrong closet. Then when we tried to dangle him and make ghost sounds, the wind picked up, and he crashed through Stephanie's window."

Ivan thought Mr. Kulecza was lucky not to have a bullet hole in the middle of his plastic forehead. He put out a tentative finger and touched the mannequin's cheek. "What about Mr. and Mrs. Platz?"

"It was a pity haunt. An act of mercy."

Stephanie knew from police work that surprise and stress were capable of distorting perception. She silently repeated that truth over and over as she rode back to Camden with Ivan.

Melody and Lucy and Ace and possibly

seven hundred other people had connived to return Haben to the Rasmussen family. Ivan had nothing to do with it, she told herself. He had proposed because he loved her. It had never occurred to him that he could regain Haben through marriage, right? Right. Why was she even thinking such trash?

She closed her eyes and leaned back in her seat. She couldn't shake the doubt. If it had occurred to all those shoemakers, it could have occurred to Ivan. She waged a mental debate. Low self-esteem, she told herself. She couldn't believe Ivan would want to marry her for herself. That was ridiculous, she decided. She liked herself. Her esteem was just fine and dandy. He'd be lucky to get a prize like her. Oh yeah? came the reply. What about Steve? He didn't want her. Stephanie smacked her forehead. Steve was *gay*, for crying out loud. He wanted Roger Beldon! She shook her head. She was getting weird. Her CPU was overloaded.

"Ivan, I need to get away for a while."

He'd known it was coming. She hadn't spoken a word since they'd left the factory parking lot, but the air had crackled with unspoken accusation and painful confusion. He knew she was waging a silent war, debating the possibility of dishonorable intentions on his part. It was understandable. His first thoughts had run along the same lines. He'd listened to Melody's explanation and suddenly felt revolted at the thought of marrying Stephanie to get Haben back.

Of course, the plan had been for them to fall in love, and that wasn't nearly so mercenary. But it had raised uncomfortable questions all the same. Questions Stephanie was going to have to answer all by herself. A good marriage had its share of blind faith. Stephanie was going to have to look inside herself and decide if she had enough faith in his love to marry him. And he was going to have to sweat it out, he thought ruefully.

Stephanie stopped for a light, stretched her cramped. arms toward the windshield, and flexed her fingers. She'd been on the road for nine hours. It seemed like nine days. She'd gone home to Jersey City to regroup and think things through, and had found out that home was no longer in New Jersey. It was nice to see her parents and friends, but she'd been a visitor. Her home was in Maine now, and she'd been anxious to return.

Anxious to return. The phrase stuck in her mind as she slowly drove through the town of Camden, over the Megunticook River, and north on High Street. She decided that anxious was exactly the right word to describe her feelings.

She'd left without much of an explanation to Ivan and wasn't at all sure what she'd find waiting for her at Haben. She'd simply said she'd needed to get away, and she'd headed south, smarting under the realization that she'd been manipulated by strangers, friends, and relatives. She'd probably looked like a blithering idiot, not even recognizing her own water heater!

By the time she'd reached New Jersey, she'd gone over every detail and was laughing out loud. The whole scheme had been outrageous. And doubting Ivan's love had been equally insane. Several times she'd started to call Ivan from New Jersey but had hung up even before she'd finished dialing. The telephone seemed inappropriate for the message she wanted to convey. Now she was going to see him, face-to-face, and she was nervous.

The nerves disappeared when Haben came

into view. Someone had decorated the front
porch with pumpkins and Indian corn, and a
cutout of a ghost had been taped to the front
door for Halloween. This is the real Haben, she
thought. It wasn't staid and stuffy, and she'd be
foolish to try to force her preconceived ideas of
stately elegance on the big old house. It was
daily disasters and fun on holidays, and it
probably really did have a ghost who broke toilets. Ivan was right when he said it was a house
that needed children and dogs and an orange
cat. She glanced down at the small ball of orange fluff sleeping on the seat next to her. It
was a step in the right direction. Maybe next
month she'd get a dog. The kids might be
harder to come by.

She pulled into the driveway, slung her
purse over her shoulder, and cuddled the kitten in the crook of her arm. She wasn't surprised to find the front door unlocked.

It all felt very right. As if the house were
waiting for her. And she knew Ivan would be
waiting for her, too, because Ivan loved her.
It was a love she would be able to count on
for the rest of her life. A love she would
return.

The foyer floor had been freshly polished,

pots of mums decorated tables and cozied up corners. The clocks ticked in cadence as if they were the heartbeat of the house. A sliver of golden light shone under the closed kitchen door. Stephanie pushed the door open and found Ivan standing at the counter, chopping vegetables. He wore khakis, a bulky sweater, and loafers. His hair had been cut and his beard shaved off, but he was still heart-stoppingly handsome and frighteningly virile. He seemed as at home in the kitchen as he'd been at the helm of the *Savage*.

"Making supper?" Stephanie asked.

He turned at the sound of her voice, the surprise apparent on his face. He recovered quickly and smiled at her, and the smile said it all. Welcome home, I missed you, I love you. It took her breath away, and she wondered how anyone could say so much with a simple smile.

"I'm making an omelet. Are you hungry?"

"Yeah." She smiled back at him. "I'm starved."

He took the kitten from her and held it up for inspection. "Is this a new boarder?"

Stephanie nodded. "It's a wing chair cat."

"What's its name?"

"Whiskers."

"Are you hungry, Whiskers?" he asked the cat, taking a bowl from the cupboard. He filled the bowl with milk and set the bowl and the cat on the floor. Then he gathered Stephanie into his arms and kissed her. "I missed you."

"I missed you, too."

"Yeah?"

She laughed softly because he was so obviously pleased. "Why isn't Lucy making supper?"

"Lucy and Melody haven't moved back. They weren't sure they were welcome."

"Hmmm. I see that didn't stop you."

"My rent is paid through May."

Stephanie wrinkled her nose. "Sorry I left in such a huff, but it was a little embarrassing to discover a whole town had conspired to get me married. I can hardly wait to get my hands on Lucy, Melody, and Ace."

"You're not mad at them?"

She twisted her mouth into a fiendish smile. "I don't get mad—I get even. Their days are numbered. At this very moment there are two handsome bachelors packing their bags in New Jersey."

"What about Ace? Isn't there a bachelorette en route to Maine for Ace?"

Stephanie shook her head. "Ace isn't ready for marriage. But when he is, I'm going to cut him down at the knees!" She raised her eyebrows at Ivan. "And I suppose you've moved into the master bedroom?"

He kissed her again. Long and sweet. "Mmmm. Aunt Tess insisted on it."

"You're pretty sure of yourself, aren't you?" she said, teasing.

His hand tightened at her waist. He hadn't been sure of anything except his love. She'd been gone for almost two weeks, and he'd awakened every morning dry-mouthed with fear that she wouldn't return. Not a phone call or a postcard, and now here she was, looking at him as if she had the world by the tail. He had a strong inclination to shake her until her teeth rattled. Instead, he kissed her hard, crushing her against him.

She slid down from the kiss and rocked back on her heels, licking tingling lips. "Maybe I'm not as hungry as I thought," she said. "Not for supper anyway."

Ivan held her at arm's length and looked at her. "Are you sure?"

He didn't have to say more. They both knew what he was really asking. Are you sure you love me? Are you sure you're ready to make a binding commitment to that love? Are you sure you don't need more time?

Stephanie gave him a big smackeroo-type kiss. *"Yes!"*

Ivan pressed his face into her silky hair and swallowed, allowing relief and joy to wash away two weeks' worth of loneliness and doubt.

Mine, he thought happily, hugging her, swinging her off her feet with a loud war whoop. He scooped her into his arms and carried her up the stairs to the master bedroom. He struck a match to the kindling that had been stacked in the black marble-and-mahogany fireplace and waited while the larger logs caught. He lit the candles in the wall sconces and turned down the thick down comforter. Then he undressed her very slowly, covering her with kisses where her clothing had been removed.

When she was entirely naked and shivering with expectation, he reached into the nightstand drawer and took out a small box. "I bought this the day you left. Sort of a token of faith, I guess."

He opened the box and removed a perfect

diamond in a simple gold setting. He held the ring between his fingers and solemnly offered it to Stephanie. "Once this ring goes on, it never comes off, Steph. Will you marry me?"

She'd always expected falling in love would be a gradual, logical process, but a pushy ghost had tumbled her down a hill—right into the arms of a pirate. And then she'd been maneuvered into bed by an entire town of backwoods matchmakers. Not your average romance, but it didn't matter. She loved Ivan Rasmussen and his haunted house and his beautiful ship and his silly shoe factory. She slid the ring onto her finger and looked into his smoky gray eyes.

"Yes, I'll marry you. But I'm not sure about sleeping in the master bedroom." She gave an involuntary shiver and drew the quilt over herself. "I have this creepy feeling we're being watched."

A gust of wind whipped through the room, the bedroom door slammed shut, and there was the soft tread of feet on the stairs to the cupola.

"Must be the cat," Ivan said.

"Maybe," Stephanie said slyly. "Maybe not."

If you were swept away by
Love Overboard
check out this sneak preview of
Back to the Bedroom
by Janet Evanovich
Available Now Wherever
Books Are Sold

There were seven row houses on the 400 block of A Street NE. Six of them were Federal style: narrow, three-story, red-brick buildings with long, arched windows and flat roofs. Each had a small false front peak imprinted with the date of construction—1881, 1884, or 1878. As was the custom at that time, basements were accessible from the front, five steps down. The first floor was five steps up. Front doors were sunk into arched alcoves, and the doors were thick oak, capped by decorative lead windows. Yards were small, minuscule actually, but packed with flowers, herbs, ivies, and stunted dogwood trees.

The residents of A Street NE used every available inch in property values. And it was inhabited by ambitious professionals. The street wasn't so wide or so heavily traveled that it couldn't be crossed to say hello. Old-fashioned globed streetlights studded the narrow margin between curb and red-brick sidewalk, casting circles of light on shiny BMWs, Jaguar sedans, Mini Coopers, and Saab 900s.

In the middle of the block, flanked on either side by its tall, dark, dignified Federal neighbors, sat a fat two-story Victorian town house. Its brick had been painted pale, pale gray, the elaborate ribbon and bow stucco trim was gleaming white, and its gray tile mansard roof was steeply slanted. The house was dominated by a rounded half-turret facade with a conical gray tile roof tipped in silver and topped with a flying horse weather vane.

It was an outrageous house, a birthday cake in a showcase filled with bran muffins. And it was inhabited by David Peter Dodd, who at first glance was neither birthday cake, nor bran muffin, nor A Street material by any stretch of the imagination. With his brown hair, brown eyes, medium build, and average height, he wasn't a man you would immediately notice, and he preferred it that way.

He was thirty-one but he looked younger, and

he was sitting on the front stoop of his house reading an X-Men comic book when a large object fell from the sky and crashed through the roof of his next door neighbor's house.

Katherine Finn, called Kate to her face and the Formidable Finn behind her back, was in her kitchen when she heard the crash. It sounded more like an explosion than an intrusion. The overhead Casablanca fan jiggled from the vibration, windows rattled, and a bedraggled hanging Boston fern broke from its moorings and smashed onto the kitchen floor. The half-empty quart of milk Kate was holding slid from her fingers. She felt her heart jump to her throat, muttered an expletive, and ran to the front door, pausing in mid stride when the house settled down to eerie silence.

Kate stood absolutely still for a moment, listening, but she was unable to hear anything over the pounding of her heart. When her pulse rate slowed back to a normal beat, allowing her some semblance of rational thought, she concluded if anything were liable to explode it would have to be in the cellar. There were things down there that made odd rumbling noises when they were working. There were pilot lights and emergency off-on switches, and an intimidating tangle of pipes and wires.

She took a deep breath, opened the cellar door, and sniffed. No smoke. She switched on the light and crept down the stairs. No fire. No evidence of explosion. She shook her head in confusion and turned to go back upstairs.

And let out a shriek when she bumped into David Dodd.

He looked at her over his wire-framed glasses and reached out to steady her. "Are you okay?"

She clapped her hand to her heart and gasped for breath. "You scared me!"

"I heard the noise, and I came to see if you were all right. The door was open. . . ." He made a vague gesture in that direction and removed his glasses.

They'd been neighbors for three months, but he'd never been in her house. In fact, he'd never spoken more than three words to her at any one time. That hadn't stopped him from forming an opinion.

He'd observed that she was a woman who moved fast and kept erratic hours. She didn't dally between her car and her front door, barely taking time to wave and mumble "hello" while she fumbled for keys. She usually rushed by him in a stern black coat that hung almost to her ankles with a huge leather purse slung over her shoulder, a grocery bag balanced on her hip, plastic-draped clothes from the cleaners caught in the crook of a finger, and more often than not she was dragging a large, odd-shaped metal case that was equipped with casters and stamped with a bunch of travel stickers.

Because he didn't know her name, Dodd thought of her as the Mystery Woman. He was fascinated by the amount of raw energy she exuded between curb and doorstep. Her impersonal, hurried hellos annoyed the hell out of him. And he hated the damn black coat.

Dave knew he was in big trouble when he started hating the coat. It was just a piece of clothing, for crying out loud. It belonged to a woman who was a virtual stranger. So what if the coat was unflattering? So what if it was missing a button on the half belt at the small of her back? It was none of his business, right? Wrong. It was driving him nuts. Clearly it was the result of having too much free time on his hands, Dave thought. He was getting weird. He had become fixated on a neighbor who wanted nothing to do with him. He'd been

251

lonely and wondered if she was lonely too.
And then he started wondering what was
under the all-concealing coat. A tweed suit? A
silky dress? Maybe nothing at all?

Now he was finally standing next to the Mystery Woman, and his heart was pounding. Normal reaction when worrying about the safety of
a neighbor, he told himself. It had nothing to do
with the fact that her complexion was flawless,
or that she had outrageous Little Orphan Annie
hair. She was smaller than he'd originally
thought. About five feet five and delicately
boned with a pixieish face and large green eyes.
She was wearing a pair of baggy gray sweats
that molded to her soft curves and clung to her
small waist. David concentrated on her blue
and gray running shoes while he tried to exert
some control over his testosterone level.

She took a step backward and swiped at the
wispy curls that fell across her forehead. "I
don't understand it. Everything seems to be
okay here."

"I guess it didn't make it to the cellar."

She looked at him sideways. "What are you
talking about?"

"The thing that crashed through your roof. It
must have stopped on the second floor."

Her eyes opened wide. "Something crashed through my roof? I thought it was an explosion in my cellar."

David took her elbow and nudged her toward the stairs. "I think the only thing that exploded was your milk. It's all over your kitchen floor."

"Okay, wait a minute, let me get this straight. You saw something crash through my roof. As in 'dropped from the sky' kind of crashed through my roof?"

"I didn't actually see it so much as hear it. There was a helicopter. I remember it making those *whump, whump, whump* sounds, and then . . ." He made a whistling sound through his teeth and ended with an explosion. "Right through your roof," he concluded.

Kate pushed him aside and took the stairs two at a time. The house was only one room wide. The front door opened to a foyer, which led to the small living room. An elaborate mahogany arch separated it from the dining room, and the kitchen, surprisingly large, was at the back of the house. There were two bedrooms and a bath on the second floor.

Kate halted abruptly at the door to the front bedroom and gasped. There was a huge ragged hole in her ceiling. She looked through the hole into her third-floor attic room and a corresponding hole in the attic roof. Chunks of plaster were strewn about the room, sunlight poured through the roof, and a mist of fine powder floated in the air like fairy dust. The queen-size bed had collapsed, a scarred chunk of twisted metal lay square in the middle of the mattress.

"My Lord, what is it?" Kate asked.

David approached it cautiously. "I'm not sure, but I think it's a camera pod from the helicopter. I used to do a lot of photography. Once I did an aerial survey for a new subdivision in Fairfax County, and we had an auxiliary video camera mounted on a pod like this.

Kate felt dazed. A helicopter part had fallen through her roof. It made perfect sense. That was the sort of week she was having. On Wednesday her accountant had called to say her taxes were being audited. She'd gotten a speeding ticket on Thursday and a parking ticket on Friday. And this morning the cleaners had informed her of a "small mishap" to her favorite black coat.

It was all too much even for Katherine Finn, a master at defusing frustration. She was a professional musician, a child prodigy who'd begun auditioning at the age of seven. By the time she was twelve she'd suffered more stress, humiliation, and rejection than most people do in a lifetime . . . and she'd also reaped more rewards and more successes.

She didn't have a temperamental or mean bone in her entire body, but early on she'd learned how to manipulate, how to protect her ego, how to throw a well-aimed temper tantrum. Katherine Finn would never have a heart attack from suppressing emotion. Katherine Finn smashed plates, hugged babies, devoured food, and cried buckets at weddings, funerals, and sad movies.

"Do you know what this used to be?" she shouted at David Dodd as she furiously paced beside the bed. "This used to be a brand-new, three-hundred-dollar feather quilt. Prime goose down that was going to keep me warm this winter."

David raised his eyebrows and looked at the quilt with obvious envy.

"I suppose you think goose down grows on trees. Well, let me tell you, I worked long and hard for that stupid goose down. And now what? Who's going to pay for this?" She paused and ran a hand through her hair. "I should call someone," she said. "My insurance company, the police, the airport. Blooming-dale's linen department."

She looked up at the swatch of blue sky showing through her roof. "I need a carpenter, a roofer. Damn, it's Saturday. I'll never be able to get a carpenter out here today. What if it rains? What if word gets around about this? Degenerates and drug addicts could just drop in whenever they wanted." She narrowed her eyes and shifted from foot to foot. "Boy, I'd just like to see them try. I'd be on them like white on rice."

David believed her. She had that tight-lipped, don't-mess-with-me look a Doberman gets when he hasn't eaten in three days. Her eyes were a flash of emerald green. Her hair seemed electric. She was getting hysterical, he decided. And she was magnificent. He picked up the bedside phone and dialed.

"Who are you calling?" Kate asked. "The police?"

"No, the pizza place on the corner. You look like you could use lunch."

For the life of him, David couldn't figure out why he wanted to feed this crazy person. Common decency, he told himself. He shook his head. That was a bunch of bull. He wasn't all

that decent. He silently groaned and grimly ac-
knowledged that he was hooked. Now that he
knew what was under the awful black coat,
there was no turning back. Now he wanted to
get rid of the gray sweats. He wanted to get rid
of them *bad*.

Kate looked at the man standing in her
bedroom and realized she didn't know his
name. Although he'd moved in three months
earlier, she'd never introduced herself. She
was a lousy neighbor. She probably should
have baked him a cake or something. She'd
practically snubbed him, and he'd still
rushed over to help her when disaster struck.
A nice person, she thought. And he was or-
dering pizza! A little offbeat, but thoughtful.
"Is pizza your standard remedy for hysterical
women?"

He hung up the phone and plunged his
hands into the pockets of faded jeans that had
a hole worn through at the knee. He was wearing a blue and black plaid flannel shirt draped
loose over a navy T-shirt, and he was standing
on his heels in new white tennis shoes, watching her. "No, but I thought it might be too soon
for brandy."

"You mean too early."

257

"Mmmm. Too early."

Not only didn't she know his name, but she wasn't sure if he was married. She had never seen him go off to work, and she was surprised at how attractive he was. From a distance he'd seemed loose-jointed and boyish, but at close range he had a compact, muscular body. He was about five-eleven with corded arms, a flat belly, and eyes that were a deep, rich brown. The eyes didn't miss much, and they didn't give away much, she decided. Nothing more than he wanted. They were intelligent and perceptive. He had a wide, firm mouth that looked a trifle stubborn but held a hint of humor.

"I don't think we've actually met," she said, holding out her hand. "Katherine Finn. Everyone calls me Kate."

"David Dodd."

"I've been a crummy neighbor."

"Yup."

Kate raised her nose a fraction of an inch. It was an intimidating gesture she used when put on the defensive, a habit developed after years of coping with four brothers and countless arrogant, eccentric music teachers.

Dave grinned at her. "Nice try, but haughty

isn't going to work. You should have baked me a cake. Emily Pearson, across the street, baked me a cake. And Mrs. Butler, in the corner house, baked me a cake."

Kate controlled the impulse to make a face and say something rude about Emily Pearson and Mrs. Butler. They were nice people. And they made her crazy. Their windows were always spotless. They put up appropriate door ornaments for Halloween, Thanksgiving, and Christmas. They baked fruitcakes for neighbors and made chicken soup for sick people. For a woman who once left her Christmas lights up until July and didn't own a pie plate, they were a hard act to follow.

"I was going to bake you a cake, but I just never got around to it."

"It's not too late. You could bake me a cake today."

"Don't get pushy."

The grin widened. "Just trying to be helpful. I didn't want you to carry around a load of unnecessary guilt."

"Very thoughtful of you. The truth is, I'm not much of a baker."

He slung his arm around her shoulder and guided her out of the bedroom, down the stairs. "Hey, you can't let that stop you. Baking isn't so tough. I happen to have a no-fail layer cake recipe that'll knock your socks off. Since you're obviously not the domestic type, I'll make the cake and—"

Kate dug her heels into the runner. "Hold it," she said, hands on hips. "What do you mean, 'obviously not the domestic type'?"

"Domestic types always know how to bake cakes." He stood at the foot of the stairs and looked around at the bare living room and dining room. "And domestic types usually own furniture."

Kate followed his gaze around the two rooms. "I'm divorced. He got the furniture, and I got the house payments." As she appraised the empty living room, she pushed her hair behind her ears, but it immediately sprang forward to its original position.

"I suppose I could use a chair or something, but I haven't much money left over at the end of the month." She seemed lost in her own thoughts for a moment while she remembered how the house had looked filled with Anatol's furniture. Sleek black leather and gleaming chrome stuff that she'd hated. "Of course, it's easier to vacuum this way," she concluded.

"I'm sorry about your divorce."

She made a dismissive gesture. "We're still friends. We just weren't destined to live together. We drove each other crazy. The divorce didn't signify failure, but a truce."

"So you're hard to live with, huh?"

"I'm impossible."

"I'm easy to live with," he announced as he followed her into the kitchen. "I'm very likable."

She raised her eyebrows. He was likable all right. He was so likable it was frightening.

He took a cookie from the open bag on the kitchen counter. "Don't you think I'm likable?" He knew he was likable. He'd made a whole career out of being invisible and likable. It was a natural talent. "You sound a little cynical about it." He munched on the cookie, surprised that the cynicism had crept out. "It's a curse."

"Uh-huh." Kate dropped a kitchen towel onto the floor and sopped up the milk. "You want to call the police or you want to clean the floor?"

He reached for the wall phone. "No contest."

An hour later, they'd finished their pizza and an FAA investigator had arrived. They led him up to the bedroom. "So," Kate said hopefully, "anyone report a missing piece of metal?"

The man paled and swore softly at the

wreckage. "I'm glad you're not a late sleeper." He photographed the ceiling and the bed and returned with a packing crate. "We'll be in touch as soon as we get this straightened out."

A representative from Kate's insurance company arrived fifteen minutes later.

"Heard on the weather report that it's supposed to rain," he said, looking at the hole in Kate's roof. "Supposed to get colder too."

Kate peered up at the patch of sky showing through her ceiling and groaned. It really wasn't fair that misfortune had singled her out. She wasn't such a bad person, she thought. A little disorganized and maybe just a teensy bit self-centered. So she wasn't such a great neighbor, but hey, she'd been busy. And it wasn't as if she'd been an *awful* neighbor. She was quiet most of the time, and she usually parked in her own parking space, and she almost always said hello to him. . . .

The alarm rang on her bedside clock. Simultaneously, an alarm went off in the kitchen. Kate smacked her forehead with the heel of her hand. "Oh, damn!"

Dave reached for the clock. "What's going on?"

"I'm late!" Kate rushed to her closet and grabbed a garment bag. "That's my late alarm.

I'm awful with time. When the alarms go off it means I have only half an hour to get to the Kennedy Center and dress. Special matinee today. I knew I'd forget!"

She snagged her big leather purse from the dresser and took off at a dead run. She got halfway down the stairs, turned, and popped back into the bedroom. "Dave, can you take care of this for me? And lock up the house when you leave. And thanks for the pizza."

She was gone. Dave and the insurance man stared out the open bedroom door in silence, unconsciously holding their breath. They resumed breathing at the sound of a car being gunned from the curb.

The insurance man blinked and smiled in amazement. "Is she always like this?"

"Probably.'

By the time Kate returned, it was pouring. She dashed from her car and huddled in the dark alcove of her front door, searching through her purse for her key.

The concert had been followed by a mandatory reception and dinner that had seemed interminable. She'd cracked her knuckles when the consommé was served, tapped her foot relentlessly through the chicken almondine, and bolted down her poached pear in raspberry sauce. When rain had softly pattered against the windows, a variety of emotions had run through her. She'd been relieved that it wasn't a good night for rapists to go prowling around looking for houses with holes in their roofs, concerned that, in addition to everything else, she now had water damage—and an undeniable yearning for David Dodd's no-fail layer cake.

She shivered as rain drizzled down her neck and soaked into the back of her sweats, and she wistfully longed for the black coat the cleaner had destroyed. The coat had been like Little Bear's porridge. Not too hot, and not too cold. It had always been just right. Not too long, not too short. It had fit her perfectly. And now it was gone . . . just like her roof. Damn.

She wedged her music case between her leg and the door, protecting it from the elements out of habit. She found the key and let herself into the foyer, for the first time in her life feeling slightly insecure in her own house. Her haven, her sanctum sanatorium, was vulnerable. It had been violated by a pod. Whatever that was.

"A pod!" she said aloud. "A big, stupid pod."

She shook the rain from her hair and apprehensively trudged upstairs, hating the feeling of doom that had descended on her since she'd entered the house. Don't get paranoid about this, she told herself. It was one of those once-in-a-lifetime freak accidents, and now that she'd gotten it out of the way, the coast was clear. She was in good shape for the next hundred years. Still, it was creepy to have something drop out of the sky into your bed.

She switched the light on in her bedroom and pressed her lips together at the sight of the quilt. It looked dead. It smelled like wet fowl, and water dripped from the ceiling with a depressing *splat* onto the soggy lump of torn coverlet and massacred feathers.

Something thumped overhead. Footsteps on her roof. The sound of a heavy object being dragged toward her. She searched for a weapon, finding only a hairbrush, flannel nightgown, empty yogurt cup. In desperation her hand closed around a cut-glass perfume atomizer.

"Whoever's up on my roof better not come any closer," she announced and aimed the atomizer at the hole. "I've got Mace."

David Dodd peeked over the edge and grinned down at her. "That's not Mace. That's a perfume atomizer. The best you could do with that is strip me of my masculine body odor."

"You have to use your imagination."

"Uh-huh."

She squinted into the darkness of the third floor. "What are you doing up there?"

"Trying to fix your roof. I'd have had it fixed sooner, but I had to drive all over town trying to find a big enough piece of plastic." He disappeared and a slab of wooden slats was shoved halfway across the opening.

Kate recognized it as a section of the six-foot-high privacy fence that divided their backyards.

"Hope you don't mind that I used part of the fence," he said, inching it into place. "It's hard to get a lumber delivery on Saturday night."

He walked around the perimeter of the hole and reached forward to tug the wood into place. Then there was the sound of tarred paper tearing and David Dodd dropped like a stone, through the hole in the roof, through the hole in the second-floor ceiling, and landed with a *whump* that knocked the air out of him, flat on his back, spread-eagle on the soaking wet, smashed-in bed.